TANGLED IN THE
Web

CHECKMATE

CHARLEE BRAVO

TANGLED IN THE WEB: *Checkmate* by *Charlee Bravo*
Published by Charlee Bravo Productions
Philadelphia, Pennsylvania
www.charleebravoproductions.com

Cover by Kamile Kuntz
Design and Formatting: Nonon Tech & Design

ISBN: 979-8-9855325-7-9
July 2024
Printed in the United States of America

This is a work of fiction. Any reference or similarities to actual events,
real people, living or dead, or real locales are intended to give the novel a
sense of reality. Any resemblance in other names, characters, places, and
incidents is entirely coincidental.

TABLE OF CONTENTS

ACKNOWLEDGMENTS

Team Tangled… Its been 2years & 3books later… Prayers are being answered. I trust the process and believe that one day our TANGLED IN THE WEB book series will not only be in your hands to read, but WE will be in theatres all across the world… I'M ROLLING THE DICE & I'M BETTING ON MYSELF!!!!! I'm BOLDLY speaking it into fruition, praying that the universe will hear me.

This book/author journey has been an uphill battle, but thankfully it has gotten a pinch easier since we first started in 2010,

yet there is always something new to learn. I'm so grateful that God has placed the right people in my life because (real talk) all I can do is write....LOL, it is NO SECRET that I'm technology-challenged I don't even know how to, copy & paste SMDH. But what I have done, is found some phenomenal people who excel in their crafts and together we have once again published another page-turner. Thank you to everyone OLD & NEW who has assisted in any kind of way big or small, your input was most appreciated....xoxo

A special thank you to Sean, you are the epitome of an AMAZING HUSBAND...Hands down you are the best at multitasking and keeping my head in the game, between you and my editor-in-chief Monica, there was only one option, GET IT DONE!!!!!! XOXOX

Thanks again to my daughter Ciara, Toni & my mom Chris for the extra help xoxo. Scooty, Yani, Desharne, Michelle, Danny, Aunt Khaleelah & Aunt Monica as usual y'all held it down for both book launches of 2022 & 2023 along with my sons Mark, Lil Sean, & Derek. I truly appreciate all of the love & support, both events were EPIC!!!!! Xoxoxo

Thanks to my extended book team.
Janette Lewis ...Manuscript Typist
Monica Harmon...Editor

Kamile Kuntz …Graphic Designer
Lebanon Raingam….Formatter
Marcell Clark…. Photographer
Lisa Naomi….Book Adviser
Nia Davis …Website Designer
POLO…..Business Consultant
My PR Team @ ISH &CO.
Ismail….Founder
Maha Khan….PR & Marketing Operations
Arif….Creative Director
Zada….Video Editor
Khadeeja…Marketing Manager
Wasi Anwar….Digital Marketer

Thank you for all of your help with social media, and getting my magazine articles published. I truly can't wait to thank all of these team players when I'm accepting my Oscar for BEST MOVIE…

Sincerely,
CHARLEE BRAVO

INTRODUCTION

A Philly Obsession & A Web of Lies…..RECAP. Sweeah Evans(12) gets introduced to oral sex by her sister Lonnas', 17 y/o boyfriend Shae' Huges.

Sweeah has found herself in a few unpredictable situations as a teen. She sleeps with Shaes' friend Sean of the TRIPLE THREAT, then is brutally raped and left for dead in the bushes of the park after the Pep Rally.

Shae' eventually marries Lonna to stay close to young Sweeah, and 20 years later, Sweeah is happily married to Kyle. Both sisters have become mothers and have a good home life…OR DO THEY?

Who is Mikaylas' father Kyle or Shae'?

Delicious Dick in Disney…!!!

After 20 years, Sweeah and Shae' are both still physically and emotionally addicted to each other, still taking enormous risks while on the Disney family vacation.

The Boathouse…LAWD!!!!

The Mansion…..OH LAWD!!!!!

Who is Stix and Yasmine?

What does Ms.Ruth know?

How long has Sweeahs' best friend Mook been sleeping with her husband Kyle?

Did Sweeah survive the violent car collision?

The wait is over, flip the page and brace yourself…. Shit is about to hit the fan!!!!!!!!

Chapter 1

PLEASE WAKE UP!

The sounds of fire trucks and police sirens fill the atmosphere. The lights from the ambulance continue to fade as my eyes begin to close. I fight to keep them open as I get a glimpse of Mikaylah, who is covered in blood. That was the last visual I had before my eyes completely closed. The last words I heard were unforgettable. "We're losing her!!! Charge to 360!! CLEAR!!!"

A jolt goes through my body like electricity. I manage to gather just enough strength to squint my eyes open, and just before the doors of the ambulance close, I gasp at the sight of the crash. The 18-wheeler was on its side, and my car was crushed. I tried to speak, but no words came out as I thought to myself, my children! Where are my children? Once again, everything fades to black, and the last thoughts that I can remember are, *I'm not ready to die! I want my MeMe! I want my MeMe! Moooommmmyyyyy!!! Help me!*

I guess this is what some would call an out-of-body experience. I can see the doctors working on me. There's a lot of blood, and they are saying things about my blood pressure dropping. My pupils were fixed and/or dilated, and my pulse was weak. I'm standing beside the head doctor, begging him not to give up on me. I try to tell him I'm not ready to die. I want to fight. I have a family, and they need me. I then walk over to myself and say, *Sweeah Evans, you better not give up. We can do this! We can do this!! Fight, Sweeah, Fight!*

"Blood pressure is rising. Pulse is good. She's back!" These were the words of the doctor as he looked at the fragile me on the table. Then he told the medical team, "She's a fighter! She's a real fighter!!" These were the final words I heard before everything faded again. No, I think to myself. *This is the second time I've heard these same words. The first time was when I was brutally raped in the park during the pep rally.*

Shortly thereafter, "Oh Reverend! Thanks for coming. How have you been?" asked MeMe as she gently embraced the man of God.

"Liz, the question is, how have you been holding up? I know this has been taking a toll on your mind, body, and soul. But yes, Liz, continue to pray and ask God to give you strength, the same strength Jesus had to rise from the grave with all power in His hands! Ask, and you shall receive. It's been hard to see your daughter unconscious for the past six weeks, but the Lord will bring her through."

As MeMe ponders the words of the Reverend, a sweet, familiar voice so lovingly whispers, "Elizabeth Evans!!! Sweet, sweet Liz!!"

"Oh, my goodness, Evelyn!!! Evelyn! Evelyn!! Thanks for coming. What an on-time surprise!" The hugs were tight but needed. "First, how are you? Second, how is she? Any change at all?" Between seeing the Reverend and Evelyn, MeMe was overwhelmed.

"Well, she has good vitals but won't wake up. It's been a month, and I'm a wreck. The doctors say we should talk to her - but only positive things. They're unsure what she hears and what effects it could have on her if she hears something unpleasant. I wish I were in that bed instead of my baby."

"Oh, Lizzy, come here. I got you! I got you!!"

I can hear you, MeMe. I hear you!! I'm so tired and barely have enough strength to open my eyes, but I hear you! DON'T give up on me! I love you!!

Every day, I hear different voices from family, friends, coworkers, etc. I feel hugs and many forehead kisses, genuine love, and well wishes. I'm ready to wake up.

I want my life back! I just didn't know that my life as I knew it had already changed, and it was about to get worse. It's weird because I already know I'm in a coma, but why does MeMe keep talking to people in the hall? I keep hearing her say, "Let's take this outside the room."

"Good morning, love! How's my sleeping beauty doing this morning? Those were Meme's words as she brushed my hair.

"Good morning, Mrs. Evans. Your sleeping beauty just had her sponge bath; her vitals are great, and she's just been turned."

"Thank you, Nurse Whitaker. You've taken such good care of my baby during her stay here, and I personally thank you."

Thanks for giving her good reviews, Mom. She's great at body massages and making sure that I'm turned often to eliminate bed sores. Dammit! I need to get the hell up! I feel like a fucking handicap!! I need to wake up!!

"Good morning, good looking!"

I know that voice!

"Hey, Shae'! You're back already?" Meme said excitedly! I hear her voice, and it's now high-pitched. "Where's Lonna?"

Who fucking cares, I think to myself. Out of all the voices I have heard these past two months, my loving sister's voice is one of the few. When I do hear her voice, she never talks directly to me. She's always addressing other people in the room. Some sister.... But then again, who am I to judge? I definitely live in a glass house, so throwing stones is a no-no! Shit, my glass house is the one on the verge of shattering.

"Lonna's home with Amayah and Khamm. She's gonna pick Evelyn up from your house soon and wants to see Sweeah again before heading to the airport. Uncle Harvey wasn't feeling well, so she's leaving early." "Oh, Shae', I don't know if I'm coming or going. I wish Evelyn could stay."

"Mom!! Mom!! Stop – Don't cry! DON'T CRY!! She's going to wake up. She's strong, and she's not done living. She knows how much we all need her. I need her. Makaylah needs her and Khamm." His words are encouraging as he hugs Meme.

Oh God, Shae'! I miss you too! I miss you too, Mommy! Just as I feel a tear trying to form, I hear the voice of my little angel – Khamm, then Daddy, Aunt Evelyn, and Uncle Harvey on speaker, then another voice I hadn't heard in a while, my best friend, Mook. Damn, Mook!! Where have you been?

Then I hear the sweet but stern voice of Nurse Whitaker, "Hey guys, the Pastor's on his way up here, then a few of you have to hit the road." She smiled as she started pointing fingers.

I know this because I heard Shae' stand his ground as he laughed, saying, "No, don't point at me."

Then the next phrase that came out of Nurse Whitaker's mouth made every muscle in my body contract, and finally, my eyes opened as these words left her lips – and entered my ears. "Hey guys, remember… Only good news and positive conversation in here around my best patient. Maybe someone can keep her updated on the pregnancy – 16 weeks and healthy" – and just like that, my eyes opened. I couldn't believe what she had just said!

Instantly, I hear cheers, cries, and screams for the doctor to come in as Nurse Whitaker checks my pulse and my other vitals, and MeMe screams, "Thank you, Jesus!" just as the pastor walks through the door. Shae' is crying, hugging Dad, who's also crying, and instead of being happy at that very moment, I was *fucking paranoid*. All I could think about through all the noise of this exuberant celebration was… *I'm PREGNANT?! By my sister's husband or my husband?*

The tears just poured from my eyes. I couldn't believe I allowed myself to carry on and be so reckless in Disney World®. I hadn't been having sex that much with Kyle, and if my math is still at least on a 6th-grade level, 16 weeks means four months, right? I have been in a coma for two months, and we were in Disney® two months prior. *What the fuck?! No! No! No!!!*

I'm ready to go back into the coma. Shit! I'm blaming this baby on Kyle! Yup!! Don't judge me. What would you do, tell everyone you're pregnant, but not by your husband, but by your mother's son-in-law? Yeah, exactly…. Anyway, you're right. It sounds like a hot ass mess. Why doesn't Shae' look upset? He's just as happy as he can be."

Oh shit! Here he comes — here he comes! "Welcome back, stranger! Welcome back!!"

Damn! Besides the doctor, Shae' was the first touch I felt; oh my word, it felt like heaven! He touched my hair gently and bent over to give me a sensitive forehead kiss. He whispered in my ear, "Damn, I really fucked you into a coma?" I smiled as if to say, *Hell fucking yeah!*

And then it hit me…*Where's Kyle, and where did Mook go?* Because she was here not too long ago. No need to look for Lonna. I just heard Mom say Lonna had just taken her prescriptions to get filled for her eye. It hasn't been the same since the bug fucked her up in Disney World®.

Okay, my husband's not here, my best friend has slipped out, and I still haven't seen any of my children since I opened my eyes. I can't wait to see all of them. Makaylah, KJ and Khamm and my niece, Amayah.

I try to speak, but my voice is a little slurred. "MeMe! MeMe! Where's the kids?" I say in a groggy whimper. "I wanna see the kids."

"Oh baby, calm down. Just relax. The children are fine. Let's make sure you're okay. Khamm just left with Mook before you woke up."

I scream as the pain hits my head like a freight train. Flashes fill my head with visions of me and the kids going school shopping at Walmart.

"Sweets! What's wrong? Evelyn, get the doctor! Hurry! Hurry!!"

Pastor hurried over, grabbed my hands, and started praying over me. The pain hit again. BOOM!! I grab my head as the doctor rushes in and asks for the room to be cleared. He checks me and puts something in my IV to ease the pain and the anxiety.

"Sweeah," he says, rolling his stool over to the bed. "Do you remember how you got here? Or who brought you here?"

"No. No. Just school shopping at Walmart. That's it."

"Okay. Okay. Relax. Give your memory time to come back. I'm sure this is temporary."

I couldn't remember anything but school shopping, which was becoming a blur as I started feeling more at ease. The meds they put in my IV drip must be kicking in because my eyes start to slowly close, and I can't fight it. As I sleep, I can't help but dream about me blaming this baby on Kyle, then the baby needing a blood transfusion, and Kyle finds out not only is he not the daddy, but Shae' is a perfect match. *What the fuck am I gonna do?* But wait, something's a little off. When I asked Mom about the kids, why didn't she congratulate me on being pregnant? Those are my thoughts as everything fades. Maybe she doesn't know – that statement woke me up.

Chapter 2

TRUTH HURTS

" "I'm not sure she's ready," says Kyle.

"She's not strong enough, doctor," says MeMe.

"Yeah, Doc – God forbid she slips back into a coma. Then what?" says Dad.

"Mr. & Mrs. Evans, it's not likely that she will slip back into a coma. She's been getting stronger every day. And, sir, your wife is a fighter! She needs to learn – accept – digest – and come to grips with everything that has happened since the day of the accident. The longer you wait, the worse it could be. She could even resent all of you for holding back all of this information. We have social workers, psychologists, psychiatrists, and all the professionals your family may need. And if it makes you more comfortable, we can have one of them explain to Sweeah what happened. Either way, she needs to know the truth. It's unclear how she may react, so for Sweeah's well-being, I would suggest having one of our professionals present if one of the family members thinks she will take the news better from you guys. The choice is yours."

Okay! Okay! What the fuck is going on? I try to lay still as I hear most of this four-way conversation between the doctor, my mom and dad, and Kyle. I just found out there was an accident, and from what I'm hearing, it may have been my fault, and no one knows how to tell me. So, I'll tell them.

"MeMe. MeMe. Come over here."

"Oh, good morning, Sweety! Kyle and Dad just stepped out. They'll be right back."

"Good morning, Ms. Sweeah Evans. How's my favorite patient doing today?"

"Hey, Nurse Whitaker. I'm okay." I say in a low tone. "Nurse Whitaker, can you please raise my headrest? I'm a bit uncomfortable."

"Of course, Sweeah. No problem."

"Wait! Let me help you." MeMe offered.

As the head of the bed began to sit me upright, I boldly asked, "Did I cause a traffic accident? The last thing I remember was school shopping at Walmart, and I had to drive there. Now I'm here." The look on MeMe's face and the look on Nurse Whitaker's face was overwhelming, and I started screaming, "Tell me! Was there an accident? How did I slip into a coma? And if it was that bad, how did my baby survive? Talk to me!! Somebody, please tell me!!"

"Okay, Sweeah. Calm down! I'll tell you. I'll tell you, Sweets! Please calm down. Let me get the doctor, Kyle, and Dad."

As Mom left the room, I looked at Nurse Whitaker, and through all my tears, I reached out for her hand. "Can you tell me the truth? What the fuck is going on? I mean, I'm not that stupid. My family has been acting out of the norm since I was in the fucking coma. I heard bits and pieces, but nothing concrete because they always go into the hall, but something's wrong. During my two months in a coma, I barely heard my husband's damn voice. Was he *NOT* by my side daily? Where are my children?"

"Sweeah, listen. Listen to me!!! I will tell you what happened and will answer any questions you have, but your family may want to talk to you themselves…"

"NO! I want straight answers. No sugar-coated beat-around-the-bush bullshit."

"Okay. Let me get the doctor. Don't move! Stay in the bed, Sweeah. What happened next led to a semi-nervous breakdown and major depression. Are you ready? Brace yourself!"

As the tears continue falling down my cheeks, the door opens, and Mom, Dad, Kyle, Nurse Whitaker, and three doctors come in. Two of them are shrinks according to their ID badges on their lab jackets. As the first shrink introduced herself, Shae entered the room, panicked by all the doctors. He asks in a concerned voice, "What's going on?"

Dad simply says, "Shae', it's time she knows about the accident." Shae's face said it all. *I knew something was wrong.*

"Sweeah, my name is Dr. Waters. I'm a clinical psychologist, and my job is to…"

I quickly interrupted her, "Doctor! Doctor! Doctor!" with my hand up like 'hold it right there.' "Listen, I don't mean to be rude, but you can cut the bullshit and get right to the truth. I don't need a rundown on any of your job descriptions," I say out loud for the other doctors to hear. "I just need to know what the hell happened! I need to know the truth. I need it all at one time. I need someone in this damn room to break the code of silence and tell me what the fuck happened!" I yelled as more tears fell, and my fist hit the sheets. "WHAT HAPPENED??!!"

"I'll tell you." Shae' said as he stepped forward through the crowd. "You said you remember school shopping at Walmart. Well, when you left, you were upset about something. You weren't paying attention. You must have blown through a red light or something because you collided with the 18-wheeler."

SILENCE.

Now I notice that as Shae' is talking, he's walking towards me. MeMe is crying hysterically as one of the shrinks starts to hug her. Kyle yells, "I can't do this!" and leaves the room. Dad chases after him. Nurse Whitaker encourages Shae' to continue. Shae', who is now holding my hand, says, "Sweeah, the accident was bad. You barely made it. They had to resuscitate you."

"Wait… Wait… If I barely made it, how did my baby survive? I'm 16 weeks pregnant. I heard Nurse Whitaker say talk to me about the baby."

Nurse Whitaker quickly says, Oh no, Sweeah!! No! No! You misunderstood me. You're not pregnant, sweetheart. Mikaylah is pregnant. I was telling your family the baby was doing very well, and maybe they could share that news with you.

"Wait! Shae, what does she mean? Is Mikaylah pregnant?!"

"Sweeah, let me finish, and then I'll answer all your questions, okay? Just let me speak.

As Shae' tries his best to continue talking, I'm numb. I mean, I'm in shock, thinking about when and where my daughter got pregnant, but at the same time, I'm grateful that it ain't me! These are my thoughts until my focus shifts back to Shae', who is now stuttering over his words and crying harder than MeMe. All I hear is, "He's Gone! We lost him!"

"Shae'! Who? Who's gone? Oh my God! Did I kill the truck driver? I killed the driver?" I start to scream as MeMe runs over to console me. "Sweets!! Look at me!

LOOK at me!! Listen…" She looks me dead in my face while placing each hand on my cheeks. Baby, we lost KJ. Your son!!! He's gone!!!

Life as I knew it no longer existed. My family was distraught and torn. Some were standing by my side, while others were blaming me for the death of my son. Little did I know that the accident wasn't totally my fault, and I had no idea that those little flashes of memories would eventually start making sense. I now remember Mikaylah feeling sick in Walmart. I figured out that she must've gotten pregnant in Disney® while out with the whore, Chloe, Evelyn's damn granddaughter. Who's the father? So many questions. I can't even think straight. It's so much to digest.

All of this was going through my mind when Shae' said in a gentle voice, "Sweeah, I'm so sorry, but I couldn't tell you until the doctor gave the okay until we thought you were strong enough to handle it." I look around the room with silent tears falling down my cheeks. All I could say was, "Are you sure? Maybe he hasn't woken up yet, like me. I just woke up! Are you sure?" I looked at MeMe and then back at Shae'. "Are you sure?" I didn't realize that my reaction was so calm because as Shae' was bracing me for this news, Nurse Whitaker took the safe route and put something in my IV drip.

Chapter 3

IS IT ALL MY FAULT?

I opened my eyes a few hours later, realizing I had fallen asleep. Instantly, the tears began to fall again as I realized that what I thought was just a bad dream was indeed my reality. When I finally wiped away the tears and started to focus, I was handed a Kleenex®, and I heard a familiar voice say, "Sit up, honey. Come on, let me help you up."

"Ms. Carla?"

"Yes, baby. It's me," as she gave me a much-needed embrace.

"Ms. Carla!" I cried as she held me in her arms and stroked my hair. "He's DEAD, Ms. Carla! My baby is dead! I killed my baby!!" The tears that soaked her shirt didn't bother her as she instructed me just to let it all out, and with every stroke of my hair, she reminded me that this wasn't my fault. It was the Lord's plan, and we shouldn't question God's decisions. This was already in God's plan, and KJ was now playing on the golden streets in heaven. Shae's mother always treated me like a daughter. She was a straight-up person, and I always liked that about her. She said, "I want you to get out of bed, Sweeah. Are you strong enough?" Yes, I was out of bed before, courtesy of Nurse Whitaker, so I knew I could get up. She said, "I talked with the family and told them to get themselves together." She then continued asking me if I had any questions because she would answer them honestly.

At that moment, my brain froze. Normally, I would have a million questions, but all I wanted to know was, "Who's still blaming me?"

She boldly said, "Your husband!" She said, "Sweeah, we all want to know what could've made you so upset that you would leave Walmart and drive away recklessly. Mikaylah said although she was feeling sick and balled over, she saw tears in your eyes and heard sniffling like you were crying. She said she kinda thought maybe you had figured out she was throwing up because she was pregnant, and that had you upset."

"No! No! Ms. Carla, that's crazy! I had no clue Mik was pregnant. Shit, I thought I was pregnant!"

"What? Sweeah, your old ass?! Really??"

That gesture allowed me to laugh a little.

"Yeah, I know," I said in relief. Little did she know if I were, it would've been her grandkid.

After I was up and halfway looking human, Ms. Carla stepped out of the room and returned with a wheelchair.

As she helped me into the chair, I just broke down crying again. "It's like this is a sick joke that people are playing on me!"

She said, "Baby, it's going to be alright. But you have the right to grieve. Everyone else has already been through this phase, so just let it out."

When the wheelchair finally stopped, she opened another hospital room door and pushed the chair inside; that's where I saw my pregnant daughter sleeping in the bed. At that moment, any anger or disappointment I had with her disappeared. I was grateful she was alive, and Ms. Carla said, "The Lord may have called KJ home, but look at the blessing growing inside your daughter." She wheeled me over to her bedside, where I couldn't fight back the tears. Mikaylah's injuries were not life-threatening, but she was critical for a while. My voice must have startled her as her eyes popped open, like she thought she was having a bad dream.

"Mik… Mik… Can you hear me, baby? It's me! It's Mom!"

Tears filled her eyes as she said, "Mommy… You're really woke. Mommy… I'm so sorry. I'm so sorry. Mommy, please don't be mad."

"Baby, it's okay. It's okay, sweetheart." I motioned to Ms. Carla to help me stand up. I then leaned over top of her to kiss her face.

"Mikaylah, calm down. I'm not mad. I'm not, sweetheart." Tears fall again as I place my hand on her belly. "You're gonna be a mom! I'm gonna be a greasy grandmom!" That statement allowed all three of us to laugh.

Ms. Carla added her two cents, "You know, this baby better be born with a head full of hair, or ya' mother's gonna have a fit!"

As Mikaylah wipes her own tears, she smiles, "Well you two have nothing to worry about. This boy gives me plenty of heartburn. Mom, you always say that's a sign a baby has hair, right? Mom. Mom?"

"Sweeah, are you okay?" Ms. Carla asked, sounding concerned. My silence scared them both.

"It's a boy? It's a boy?" I asked.

Relieved, Mikaylah replies, "Yes. The last ultrasound confirmed it, and he's 'ALL BOY,' you can see 'IT'!"

Ms. Carla cracked up. "Oh, IT, huh?"

As I stroked Mik's hair, I finally answered her. "Yes, baby. Heartburn equals hair." We all laughed at my manmade theory. When the door opened, it was Mik's nurse.

"Well, well, well… Who do I have the pleasure of meeting?" she said pleasantly.

"This is my mom and my Godgrandmom," answered Mikayalah.

The nurse laughed. "My name is Ciara. Can I be a party pooper and ask you guys to step aside while I take

Ms. Evans' vitals?"

"Sure. Sure. Let us get out of your way." That's when she noticed the hospital band and me sitting in a wheelchair.

"Mom, you're also a patient here?"

"Yes. That's correct." I responded, shaking my head.

"Um, does your doctor know you're out and about?"

Ms. Carla interceded again. "No worries, Ciara. We have permission, and we don't plan on staying much longer. We know they both need their beauty rest." We didn't want to say I'm a coma patient who just found out one of my children died, and my other child is with a child. Nevertheless, while talking to us, she managed to finish Mikaylah's vitals, but then all the bad news I had received today temporarily faded as music filled the room. It was my grandson's heartbeat. Loud and strong, I released happy tears for the first time in a long time! Wow! Mik's got a little linebacker in there!

"Mom. GG (Godgrandmom), come feel him move around."

Ciara laughed, "Well, Ms. Evans, you may feel everything, but others may not feel anything for another month until his kicks get stronger."

"Stronger?" asked Mikaylah incredulously. "You mean more than this?"

"Yes, Mik. You ain't seen or felt nothing. You just

wait!"

Everyone laughed, and then Nurse Ciara kindly said, "Well, Mom, GG, Ms. Evans needs her rest, and I'm sure you need to be back in bed yourself, Mom."

"You're right. Five minutes… please?"

"Okay, ladies. FIVE minutes."

I thought to myself as I was wheeled back to Mik's bedside, 'Should I mention the loss of KJ just to see how she's handling things?' but I decided this moment was too happy and too precious, and I wanted her to go to sleep happy, not sad. I would address KJ another day. I then assured Mikaylah that I truly loved her and that I was beyond excited about my grandson, and again, that everything would be okay. I kissed her, then the baby. Ms. Carla did the same.

Mikaylah then grabbed my hand and said, "Mommy – three things you always said: 1) Heartburn = hair, 2) You can't appreciate good things if you never experience bad things, and 3) What doesn't kill you….?"

Wow! I shook my head, smiled, and replied, "Makes you stronger!!"

"I love you, Mom." Then she whispered, "It was not your fault, Mom."

Damn, she just gave me a beautiful reality check. As GG gently said, "That's my girl," then ran over to her Godgranddaughter for one last kiss and reassured her we would return tomorrow. I couldn't contain my emotions as we made our way down the hall. I was overwhelmed and grateful to know that my daughter didn't blame me for her brother's death. I was thankful that my grandson was gonna be alright, and I was indebted to Ms. Carla for making this evening possible.

Chapter 4

GOING HOME!

A fter Sweeah finally gets home, MeMe has a small welcome-home celebration for her and Mikaylah. Close family and friends enjoyed the intimate feast Momma Evans prepared for the two patients and their hungry guests. It was nice, but at times awkward because some of the guests weren't sure how to address Sweeah or Mikaylah. No one wanted to be insensitive, and often, some of the guests would check themselves if they laughed.

Noticing this, Sweeah affectionately said, "Can I have everyone's attention? I want to thank everyone for coming out. Thanks, MeMe, for all that you do. I also want to let you all know that Mik and I are okay, physically and emotionally. We are in recovery, but it's okay to laugh and enjoy yourselves. No one has to walk on eggshells. We (as she grabs Mikaylah) are okay!"

"Cheers to that!" says her happy-ass friend, Perry, as he yells, "Let's raise our glasses of juice to the two mistresses of the ceremony." Clapping and a lot of much-needed laughter fill the room. At this very moment, all the built-up tension leaves the air. As I look around the room, everyone is mingling and finally sincerely enjoying themselves, except Kyle! He's just standing against the wall, holding his glass of water. Then, he finally raised his glass up to me, and his lips softly whispered, "Murderer!"

BOOM! I instantly get a migraine. BOOM! A flashback – I'm in Walmart talking to Ms. Heath.

"Sweeah, are you okay? What's wrong?"

"I'm okay, Perry. Thanks. I need to sit down. My head is hurting." I notice Perry walk over to Kyle, say a few words, then walk back to me. "Perry, what did you say?"

"I asked him if he knew that you were still his fucking wife? Clearly, he saw you struggling, and he just stood there. It's no secret that he blames you for KJ's death! But, dammit, know this, NONE OF US DO!!! If he's gonna be a dickhead, then why even attend this celebration. Fucking loser!"

"Thank you, Perry. You know I love you!"

"And you know I got ya' back, Sweeah!"

The sun is shining so bright, and my entire bedroom is lit up. I roll over and nearly crush Khamm, who is literally stuck to my back. I take in the moment; tears fill my eyes as I silently say, 'No more brotherly fights, no more telling on each other, no more KJ!!' I switch positions so that I'm now cradling Khamm. 'He's so innocent.' I think to myself as I stroke his head. Then I think back to yesterday's party. I recall MeMe saying some guests had come but left before I arrived, but they all signed the guest book and left gifts.

"Good morning, sleepyhead Khamm and good morning, Sweets!"

"Good morning, MeMe."

"Good morning, Grandmom."

"Khamm…. You're woke?" I asked, tickling him.

"Yes! Yes! Yes! I was fake sleeping while you rubbed my face and stroked my hair."

"Boy! You're a mess!!" I said as he jumped out of the bed to run and pee. "That boy is a hot mess. A hot mess!" I said to MeMe. "How does he seem to you? He rarely talks about KJ. How do I know if he needs help if he always seems okay?"

"Sweeah, you have to remember, while you were in the coma, he grieved, and he also had counseling. Maybe he's just happy to have you and Mikayla home, and if you're still concerned, we can start his sessions back again."

"Yes, MeMe. Let's do that ASAP."

"Okay, baby. I'll call the doctor today."

"Thanks, MeMe. Oh, MeMe? Listen, did Mook come past early yesterday before I got here?"

"No. No, I don't believe so. Why?"

BOOM! The pain this time was beyond unbearable!

BOOM!! I grab my head and scream in agony. MeMe yells for Mikaylah to come into my room.

"Mikaaayyylllaaahhh!!!! Come here NOW!"

"MeMe, what's going on with my mom?"

"I'm not sure. Keep an eye on Khamm. I'm taking your mom to the ER."

BOOM!! Lights out.

Hours later

"Where am I?" I ask as my eyes open to an unfamiliar scene.

"Hello, Sweeah. You're back in the ER. You seem to have blacked out after suffering some severe headaches. What's the last thing you remember?"

"Being in bed with my son this morning."

"Okay," the doctor said. "We're going to run some tests and see if we need to keep you overnight."

"Okay," I said as I stared at the doctor, feeling like I knew him or heard his voice before. I'm sure there were several doctors in and out of my room during the two months of being in a coma.

"Hey, Sweets," MeMe said as she re-entered the room. Mikayla and Khamm are fine, and while I was in the hall, I called the pediatric therapist and got Khamm an appointment."

"Great. Thank you so much for calling. Hey, MeMe,

the doctor that just left out, was he one of the doctors that treated me while I was in my coma?"

"Oh, Sweets, you had a few doctors come and go in those sixty days. But honestly, he doesn't look like any of the doctors I saw. Why?"

"No special reason. He looks familiar, and his voice sounds familiar, but I didn't quite catch his name when he said it."

"Well, Sweeah, trust me. I'm sure he would've remembered you if he was one of your doctors. Besides, he's down here in the ER, so I doubt he was one of your coma doctors."

It's crazy because although MeMe talked to all the doctors, we all really remember Nurse Whitaker. Nurses are the real heroes. Then he returned to the room, asking me on a level of 1 to 10 how bad my headache was. I said, "Doctor, it's still like a 15." He laughed and repeated after me, "A 15? Wow!"

At that moment, it hit when he laughed. It was a weird, quirky laugh, and I knew I heard it before. So, I said, "Excuse me, doctor. I'm sorry. What did you say your name was again?" He apologized, "Oh, I'm sorry. My badge keeps flipping around." instantly, everything returned at once. I read his name. Dr. Trevor Pitts. Lonna's doctor from Disney®. What are the odds of him being in Philadelphia? I remember all too well at this very moment how and why I remembered that laugh because, oddly enough, when we were in Disney® and Lonna had to go into eye surgery. My sweet, precious KJ asked him if Aunt Lonna was gonna have a permanent pirate patch on her eye. Dr. Pitts let out that same quirky laugh and explained to KJ that it was only temporary. My emotions right now are mixed. I truly miss my baby, yet at this moment, I'm smiling at that precious memory.

"Hello? Ms. Evans? Do you hear me? Are you allergic to any medications? I'm going to give you something so we can get that pain level down to at least a 7 from 15. Okay?"

"Oh, yes. Sorry. I just had a brain freeze. No, I'm not allergic, and okay, please get me something strong for the pain, Dr. Pitts!"

"Yes, ma'am." He says as he's drawing my blood. It's weird. Either he's acting like he doesn't know me, or he honestly doesn't remember that we met. So let me jog his memory.

"Wait, Dr. Pitts. Before you go get the meds, I thought I recognized you!"

"Oh? Where from, Ms. Evans?"

"Orlando, Florida."

"Orlando." "Orlando." He repeated. "No, I don't think so." Instantly, his demeanor changed.

"Yes, a few months ago. You actually did eye surgery

on my sister, Lonna Hughes!"

At that point, he actually looked like he was gonna lose his balance.

"Are you okay, Dr. Pitts?" MeMe said. "Be careful before you fall."

"Oh no, Ms. Evans. I'm fine, thanks. I just lost my footing."

Clearly, I hit a nerve because his body language had changed. So, I kept talking. "Yes! I'll never forget you because before my son passed, you were actually the last doctor he saw, and you laughed at his curiosity about his aunt wearing a permanent pirate patch on her face."

"Oh yes! Yes. I remember now. The young lady with the bug in her eye."

"Yes," MeMe said, laughing. "That was my daughter's way of ducking her family on vacation."

"Well, how is your sister doing Ms. Evans? Any issues after the eye surgery?"

"No. I think she recovered rather well from the surgery. I haven't really seen much of Lonna lately. Everyone's been pretty busy, but thanks for asking. When I do see her, I'll be sure to tell her that we had the pleasure of seeing you again and that you helped my headache calm down, from a 15 down to a six right now."

"Well, a 6 is great, and thank you. It's my job to help people. What are the odds of me giving medical attention to two sisters in two different states?!"

"My thoughts exactly, Dr. Pitts," said MeMe. "Are you a traveling doctor?"

"Well, Mrs. Evans, I've always worked here in Philly, but sometimes volunteer in other cities and states when there's a shortage of medical staff."

"Oh wow! That's amazing," gushed MeMe. "I know your wife must miss you when you're gone, or do you guys travel together? I used to travel with my husband sometimes for work back in the day."

He smiles at MeMe. "I'm single, Mrs. Evans, so I'm actually free to move about town anyway I choose."

"Lucky you!" she said.

"I know," he replied before exiting the hospital room.

Quickly, the door reopened, and a familiar voice filled the air.

"I thought I saw your name on the board. How's my favorite patient doing?"

It's Nurse Whitaker. I nearly started crying when she extended her arms for a hug.

"Helloooooo World's BEST Nurse!!! How have you been?"

"I've been good," she replied while checking my vitals.

We all just laughed because I'm not her patient right now.

"What's this about severe migraines and blackouts?

What's going on, Sweeah?"

"I'm not sure. It's like the pain at times is unbearable, but the pain also comes with memory flashes sometimes."

"Oh, really, Sweets?" MeMe suddenly stood up and interrupted again, "Do you remember what you had so upset leaving out of Walmart?"

"No, MeMe, not yet. Flashes of me talking to Ms. Heath. Bits and pieces of the kids getting sick. That's it."

"Well, don't stress yourself out." They both said to me in unison. "That memory will come when you least expect it to, but in the meantime, some rest, diet, exercise, and therapy is what I'm recommending," said Nurse Whitaker, grinning from ear to ear.

"And call me Toni. I took care of you for so long. I feel like Nurse Whitaker is kinda inappropriate now." We all laughed. "Yes, honey. You definitely treated Sweeah like family, and she appreciated you more when she came out of the coma. You continued to encourage her physically, mentally, and emotionally, and she respected you for always being brutally honest and compassionate when she finally learned about KJ."

The room gets silent, but being the professional she is, Toni (Nurse Whitaker) turns to me and says, "Sweeah, listen. These migraines are probably more stress-related than medically related. You have to find peace with everything that happened. I know your husband blames you. I overheard so many conversations in the hallway while you were unconscious, but it wasn't my place to cuss him out. Just know that all the other visitors you had, from your hairstylist to your co-workers, no one else blames you for that accident. It was just that... a terrible accident."

At this moment, we all wipe our tears and agree that it's time to move on. She steps back and semi-yells, "So, how's the baby?"

We all laughed, and our smiles were pure and genuine.

"Oh, Toni, he's really growing! Mikaylah is getting so big, and she's glowing. He's for sure in there kicking non-stop. It's amazing to watch the process, but scary to think that one day soon, I'll be an official grandmother. Lord Jesus! I'm not ready!!"

"Well, get ready!" Toni said, snapping her fingers.

We couldn't control our laughter after that statement.

"Okay, guys, my job here is done. I put a few smiles on both of your faces, so let me finish my rounds, and here's my number. Please keep me posted on the baby. And Sweeah... I'm here for you. Seriously. Call me if you need me 'just to vent' outside of this environment. And Mrs. Evans, if you need me for anything, you also shouldn't hesitate to use my number."

"Thank you, Toni. This was way better than taking medication. I honestly felt 100% better, and at that very moment, the door opened – another nurse entered with discharge papers and a message that Dr. Pitts was called up for another emergency. He stated that your bloodwork was good and there was no need for further tests at this time.

That motherfucker just wanted to get away from me. But why? Now I'm curious.

"Okay. Thank you." MeMe said as she grabbed the papers for me to sign. "Let's go, Sweeah. I'll get the car. You can call Mikaylah and tell her we're on the way."

Chapter 5

KJ, I'M SO SORRY

Home Sweet Home is now Bittersweet Home. MeMe leaves for a second and takes Khamm with her. I sit for a moment in dead silence and pray. *'Father God, hey! It's me again, Sweeah. I want to thank you for all that you have done for me and my family. Lord, I pray that you continue to watch over all of us and keep us from dangers, seen and unseen. Lord, please keep Mikaylah and the baby safe. Keep Khamm mentally and emotionally intact. Watch over my parents; they're worried about all of us, but they need to focus on their own health. Lord, I pray that you please allow me to remember what had me so upset at Walmart that I drove off shattered and crying. And also, whatever it is, please prepare me so that I have a different reaction this time. Let me have on a full armor of God. Amen.'*

I found myself in the kitchen and yelled upstairs for Mikaylah to join me. There was still food left over, and I didn't want to 'pig out' alone. Mikaylah didn't hesitate to start heating up some chicken and sides.

"Mikaylah," I said softly, "How are you feeling?"

"I'm good, Mom. No more being nauseous during the day. I noticed that when this boy kicks, you can actually see it through my skin. It's so weird, and sometimes it hurts!"

We both laugh, and I tell her, "Oh, trust me, I know exactly what you're talking about. The bigger he gets in there, the less space he'll have to move around, and some of his movements can have you fussing and pushing on your belly, praying he changes positions."

Then she says, "It's weird being home. It's so quiet. Dad's never here anymore. My God dad hasn't been around. Aunt Lonna and my Aunt Mook are both M.I.A. What's up with all of the adults in my life?"

It was at that moment I said, "Fuck this sadness… Let's eat and watch a movie!" She agreed, and we laughed because we didn't even realize we had been standing there eating cold chicken. I guess we never heated up, but then the doorbell rings. I wasn't expecting anyone, and it was too soon for MeMe and Khamm to be back.

"Who is it?" I ask while approaching the door.

"Bitch, open up! It's me, Perry!" I lit up. Perry has that effect on me. He reached for a hug as the door opened. "I had to make sure you were okay, sweetheart." He said while looking around for Kyle.

We laughed as I said, "That fool ain't here, but damn, you smell amazing! What's the new scent?"

"It's a secret, Sweets. I'll tell you next month." We all laughed. He hates sharing his cologne names.

"We were just about to watch a movie. You want to stay and join us?"

"Of course!" he said, "But only if I can choose! Let me see what y'all have over here that's funny! Oh, YESSSSS!!! MARTIN™ DVDs. Now we are all about to laugh!"

Perry popped open the DVD case, and BOOM! My head starts to pound, and I have a flash of opening a DVD case at work.

"Sweeah, are you okay?"

"Mom, are you alright?"

"Yes. It's weird. I just had another flashback of me opening a DVD at work and then nothing. But the pain in my head is now going away, so I don't know what that was about."

Perry walks over to me and says, "Are you sure that's all you saw? Was there a name on the DVD or a color? Anything?"

"No, Perry. It honestly happened so fast. I literally just saw me opening the DVD case."

"Okay. Okay. Listen, Sweeah. This has gone on long enough, and I have a friend who is a hypnotherapist, and I'm almost positive he can help you unlock some of those memories that are trapped."

"For me and MeMe," Mikaylah says in a low tone.

"Please, Sweeah. For us. Can you give him a try?"

To their surprise and without pause, I say, "Yes! I'll go see him."

They both scream in excitement because this is a step towards victory and if Sweeah can get any extra help finding the reason for her reckless driving, she will gladly accept it.

"Now get comfy, girls, and let's get into this MARTIN™ comedy. Perry pops the DVD into the player, but as soon as it comes on, they are all in shock at what pops up on the screen. Perry jumps up off the sofa to stop the DVD.

"NO PERRY! STOP!! Let it play!!"

"MOM! PLEASE!!"

"NO MIKAYLAH! LET IT PLAY!!!"

Scared, Perry and Mikaylah sit on either side of Sweeah and watch as tears fall down her face and her nose begins to run. Sweeah whispers, "Turn it up."

"Mom! Let's not... Please, Mom?"

"Mikaylah, it's okay. Turn It Up!"

As Mikaylah aims the remote to the television to increase the sound, she hears the Reverend say, "In the short amount of time KJ was here on earth, he touched many lives..."

Sweeah sat silently as she looked at her son's body

lying so peacefully in his casket. She gets off the couch and sits on the floor directly in front of the TV.

"Mikaylah," Perry whispers, "How in the hell did the funeral DVD get in the MARTIN™ case?"

"I have no idea!" she replied, "I was in the hospital too, remember? But she was gonna see it sooner or later."

Their conversation was cut short as they could now hear Sweeah crying, "My baby. My baby."

Perry and Mikaylah join Sweeah on the floor. The choir was beautifully dressed, and they sang like angels. Sweeah said, "Oh, look! He has his favorite toys in the casket. Look at all the flowers. Look at all the pictures."

They didn't know what to say, so they agreed with everything Sweeah said. At that moment, we hear the front door open. Perry instantly got into defense mode in case it was Kyle's ass, but thank the Lord, it was MeMe and Khamm.

MeMe's face was noticeably confused. She looked at a sobbing Sweeah on the floor. 'Her baby' crying over 'her baby' – was a sight she never wanted to see again, but at this point, she knew she had to console her baby (Sweeah).

"Didn't he look like an angel?" she said as she sat next to Sweets on the floor – stroking her hair and often rubbing her back. She said in a joking way, "I put every toy I could find in his room in the prayer box (casket) so that he would be surrounded by things that made him happy."

"That was perfect, MeMe. Thanks." She said, wiping her nose on the sleeve of her shirt. "I hope to God he didn't suffer. I'm so sorry, KJ!!" she screamed as she fell completely to the floor.

"Mommy! Mommy!! Stop crying!!!" is all Sweeah heard as she felt tiny hands now around her neck. "Mommy, my brother is sleeping in heaven. If you keep crying, you might wake him up, so you have to stop crying, okay Mommy?!"

"Yes, baby. I'm sorry. Mommy forgot that we have to be quiet while KJ sleeps. I'm sorry, baby. I love you so much!" she says while hugging Khamm.

MeMe gets up, ejects the DVD, and puts on the Cartoon Channel for Khamm. Instantly, his attention was directly drawn to the TV set with the Power Rangers playing. As Perry hugged me tight, he said, "I'm getting you that therapy appointment tomorrow, so be ready. He owes me a favor, and I'm cashing in."

"Yes, mom. Please go," Mikaylah says as she walks upstairs on the cordless phone, blowing kisses and waving goodbye.

"Are you okay, Sweets? I know that was unexpected."

"Yes, MeMe. I'm fine. Strangely enough, it was just earlier today Nurse Whitaker (Toni) said things will come when I least expect them. I guess she was right."

"Well, listen," MeMe said, "I'm tired of the tears. So, what do you two think about planning a baby shower for Mikaylah? We all could use a beautiful distraction. She needs to know that although we are all still mourning KJ, we are still celebrating the life that's soon to come."

"Absolutely, MeMe!"

"Amen, Mrs. Evans. And y'all know I have a friend for everything, so I'll handle decorations." I hug my newfound bestie and laugh because he definitely has a friend for everything, including a therapist.

"Okay. So, let's all collectively figure out a good date." Sweeah said happily. "I know it doesn't seem like it, but that baby will be here in NO time!"

"Sweeah, sweetheart. Have you even talked to her yet? Who's the father? Where is he from? Since she met him on vacation, does his family even know about the baby? What's the plan for school?"

"MeMe!!" Sweeah says as she takes a deep breath. "No, I haven't even brought it up. So much has been going on. Honestly, I'm just happy my daughter is alive, and the baby is healthy. But I promise you, I'm going to sit her down and find out the answers to all of those questions."

"Okay, sweetheart. We need to know what and who we're dealing with. After all, they are still teenagers, and we don't need anybody fighting us for custody in another state."

"I totally agree 100% with your mom, Sweeah. I have an attorney friend, as well."

We all laughed, but again, we knew Perry was serious.

"Hey, Mom?" They both looked at me like crazy since I rarely ever called MeMe mom.

"What is it, Sweeah? Is it bad news? You never call me mom, even though I am. It just sounds weird."

"Again, I agree with your mother/MeMe." Perry is a low-key comedian, Sweeah thinks to herself.

"MeMe! The sign-in card from the Welcome Home party, was Mook on there?"

"Oh, Sweets, I'm not sure if Mook came. I think she told Kyle to tell the family she couldn't make it, but she would try to come to pass once you and Mikaylah got settled." Grabbing her purse, she says, "Good night, you two. See you tomorrow."

"Oh. Okay. Thanks, MeMe."

As the door closes, Perry whispers, "Go put Khamm to bed and come back down."

As I come back to the kitchen, he says, "Okay. What the fuck is going on? Where has Mook been? Is she still having a hard time after the miscarriage? Maybe seeing Mikaylah pregnant is too much for her?"

"Yeah. That's definitely possible, Perry. I'll reach out to her again in a few days. I'm trying to figure out some gut feelings that I have."

"Do tell..." Perry says with a curious look on his face. "I'm listening, Sweeah."

"It's about Lonna..."

"Oh." He said, sounding disappointed. "What about her?"

"Well, before the accident, I was at Bianca's getting my hair done when I found out that she had just recently had an abortion."

"Oh shit! Keep going." Perry said.

"And she's been hanging with these two girls, Yasmine and Stix, and coincidentally they were in Disney®.

"Never heard of them," he said.

"EXACTLY!" Sweeah blurted out. "But today, even crazier, the doctor that treated Lonna's eye in Disney® treated me in the ER..."

"Wait! WAIT!! WHAT!! He's in Philly?!"

"Exactly! Something's up, Perry. I have a feeling my sister is *Tangled in a Web of Lies!*"

"Well, after we take you to therapy tomorrow and get you all settled in, I'm calling my friend. He's a PI!"

"PERRY!"

"What? Sweeah, I can't help that I know lots of people. I NETWORK, baby!!" *Everybody needs a friend like Perry!*

They laugh as Sweeah escorts him to the door. But

then his tone changes, "Do you need me to stay in case dickhead shows up?"

"Nope. I doubt he will come home tonight. Especially if he thinks MeMe is going to be here."

"I hate his pussy ass! You know you deserve better. If I were straight, I'd wife you, boo!"

"Ha! Ha! Ha! Very funny!! I'll be fine. I'm actually feeling really good. Watching KJ's funeral gave me that closure feeling I've been searching for, and the thought of planning my daughter's baby shower has me so grateful, not to mention the hugs Khamm gave me while reminding me not to wake his sleeping brother... Yeah." Sweeah takes a very deep breath. "I'm good, Perry, and I love you!!"

"Love you too, Sweeah!"

But as fate would have it, this was the calm before the new storm. Brace Yourself!!

Chapter 6

1 – 2 – 3 WAKE UP!

I t's been a few weeks now since Perry kept his promise and introduced me to Dr. Harmon, the hypnotherapist. Our sessions started off mild, but in the last two weeks, I've been making some incredible breakthroughs, and I won't lie; at first, I was a skeptic. I really didn't believe that someone could honestly put me to sleep just by counting and talking softly, and because I was such a skeptic, Dr. Harmon insisted that we tape our sessions so I could hear myself expose what was buried in my subconscious mind.

I sit in my car and take in the scenery before my next session begins. Then I decide I have literally an hour before my session starts, so why sit in the car? I don't know why I left home so early. I guess I was giving myself extra time for traffic because therapy today is at Dr. Harmon's KOP location. Normally, I go to the Ogontz Avenue office.

It's beautiful weather today. Fall is approaching, so I grab my LV bag and jean jacket and head to the mall entrance. Now, let me be honest, I normally don't fuck with KOP™ (King of Prussia) Mall. It's too confusing. You have the mall and the court; it's just too much for me, but since I'm only going to waste time, I should be okay. Once inside, I start to smell 'Cinnabon,' and then instantly, BOOM! I grab my head, take a breath, and begin to pray… BOOM!!

Flashes of Walmart take over my mind. The same images, though, the kids getting sick, but now I see me looking at pictures of Ms. Heath's birthday party… BOOM!! I see me upset, but WHY? I try to breathe and coach myself, reminding myself that I'm in public and passing out wouldn't be a great idea. As I continue to take deep breaths, my headache starts to subside, and not a moment too soon, as my phone rings.

"Yes, Perry?"

"Did you find the KOP office okay?"

"Yeah. I got up here early, so I'm just sitting in the food court in KOP™ Mall. I honestly just had another migraine memory episode."

"Really, Sweeah? What did you remember?"

"It's crazy, Perry. I still have these Walmart® flashes, and I'm looking at birthday pics and the kids getting sick…This shit is crazy!! I NEED TO FIND OUT WHY I WAS SO UPSET WHEN I LEFT THE STORE!!! Why would I drive off so erratically?"

"Listen, Sweeah," Perry said, frustrated, "The shit's all gonna come out eventually..."

"What's gonna come out eventually?"

"NOTHING! I mean, everything! Whatever is tucked away in your pea-sized brain." He said jokingly.

"Yeah. I hope that day is today." As she said that, Sweeah got quiet.

"Sweeah. Hellooo? You there? SWEEAH!"

"Yes, I'm here. I actually remember the last time I was here in KOP was before Disney®. We had come to get KJ and Kham some Air Force Ones from the Kids Foot Locker®. That was the last time I shopped with KJ. I totally forgot about that...(silence on the phone)

"Sweeah, do you need me to come meet you? As a matter of fact, you need to head across the street. It's almost time for your session. Let me call Dr. Harmon and let the office know you're on your way."

"Thanks, Perry. I'll be okay. I'm getting myself together now and heading back to my car. I'll call you after my session."

As I stood in the lobby waiting for the elevator, I scrolled through the list of therapists and saw they also have family and pediatric counseling. Maybe Mikaylah and I can do a family session and then bring Khamm and MeMe. Fuck it! Bring everybody because it seems like everybody needs to talk about something. I just didn't know what I was about to talk about while being hypnotized today.

"Hello, Ms. Sweeah Evans!" I hear a delightful voice say with her hand extended for a mutual shake. "Do come in. My husband will be right with you."

It must be nice, I think to myself; as I enter the room, I can't help but wonder what their net income is. Shit! Two doctors, and I wonder if he ever hypnotizes his own wife?

"Hello, Sweeah! Have a seat, and let's get comfortable. Welcome to my KOP office. How are you today?

"Hello, Dr. Harmon," I say as I adjust my body in the chaise lounge. "Today has been a struggle, and I'm a bit anxious."

"Go on..." he says

"Well, my migraines are getting worse, and I keep having flashes of my day at the Walmart®, seeing Ms. Heath, looking at her birthday pictures. I see the kids getting sick, but I still can't figure out what got me beyond upset and made me drive off so recklessly with my three babies in the car. Shit... four babies, to be honest."

"Well, speaking of that... How did your conversation go with Mikaylah? Have you learned anything new about the baby's father? His family?"

"No. But I plan to. Soon."

"Sweeah. Listen. The longer you wait, the worse

things could get. It's better to find out all you can now before the baby actually arrives.

Silence fills the air.

"Sweeah? Are you okay? Why are you…"

"I saw the funeral video," Sweeah blurted out, interrupting Dr. Harmon. "I saw my baby in a casket!! I killed him! I killed him! I killed him!" Sweeah's voice kept getting louder and louder, and the tears soaked her hands as she cupped her face.

"Sweeah. Sweeah! Listen to me. Stop it!!" Dr. Harmon says as he tries to calm her down. He assured her that if she was tired of wondering, then let's dig deep today. "Relax, and let's get the answers to all your questions. We are going to DELTA! (the deep hypnosis)."

Sweeah shakes her head in agreement with what Dr. Harmon just said. He pushes a button on the phone for his wife to come in. "Our other sessions were milder; we didn't push the limits of hypnosis," Dr. Harmon says, "but I think you're ready to uncover some buried secrets."

As his wife reenters the room, she looks at a pitiful version of myself. He asks his wife if she could bring in a heated, weighted blanket.

"Are you okay, Sweeah?" his wife asked politely while handing me some Kleenex and then handed me the warm, heavy blanket.

"Yes, Dr. Harmon," I say. "I'm okay. Thanks."

She quickly interjects, "Monica. Just call me Monica."

"Thank you, Dr. Monica. I'm just a bit overwhelmed and tired and frustrated and angry and hurt, and I'm mad, and I'm falling apart, and my baby is DEAD!!!! He's dead, and I killed him!!!"

Sweeah, now collapsed to the floor and crying uncontrollably, is surprised when Dr. Monica kneels down beside her, grabbing her cheeks with one hand, lifting Sweeah's face so their eyes could meet – and with her teeth clenched tightly, she said, "Are you done with this pity party?"

Dr. Monica asked me this with a straight face. Her husband looked on in shock since he clearly wasn't expecting his wife to interfere with a professional therapy session. Caught off guard and confused, I replied, "Yes!" tears still covering my face.

"Well, get yo ass up off the floor, get back on this couch, relax your fucking mind, and find out WHY your baby died!"

Needless to say, Dr. Harmon was speechless, but he was relieved as his wife helped me to my feet, and I turned to him and said, "DELTA!"

He picked up the phone and, "Clear our schedules."

I lay across the chaise lounge, took a few deep breaths, prayed, and then requested that Dr. Monica stay for the session. Shit, they're both doctors, right? She agrees, and the session begins.

The lights are dimmed, and a refreshed, heated, weighted blanket is placed on top of me. After several minutes, I finally started to relax. Dr. Harmon's voice is now relaxed and mellow as he tries different techniques to make me comfortable. I remember him saying that it's okay to mourn the loss of my son but trying to remember that I still have two surviving children who need me, and I have a grandbaby on the way who deserves a loving, happy home.

"Listen to the sound of my voice, Sweeah. We are going back to the day. You were finally going to get school supplies for the kids. It was a workday. You had promised them that you'd take them, but first, you had to stop at the library to get KJ's summer reading book, and then you guys got to Walmart. Do you remember this?"

Let's say that was the last thing I honestly remember hearing clearly – before all hell broke loose, and I heard, "1 – 2 – 3 – Wake up!"

Chapter 7

NOW, YOU KNOW!

———————————

Dazed, I feel myself blinking and trying to focus and make out the faces in front of me. Once my vision is cleared, I can now see the look of shock and concern on the faces of Dr. Monica and Dr. Harmon.

The eerie silence both scared me and made me more curious to inquire if the Delta hypnosis worked this time. Dr. Harmon took a deep fucking breath as he got up to pour me a cup of water. Dr. Monica couldn't control her facial expressions, which made me sit up and take my own deep fucking breath. The atmosphere in this doctor's office was so tense that you could slice it with a knife. As Dr. Harmon passes me the water, he looks over at his wife and then looks back at me.

"What the FUCK is going on??!!" I blurt out. "Somebody TALK!"

I almost wish I had left well enough alone. I mean, yes, I wanted to know why I left Walmart® in such a rage that I unintentionally killed my son, but I had NO CLUE that these hypnotherapy sessions were going to unlock 'Pandora's Box.'

"Sweeah. Calm down and close your eyes."

I quickly do as I'm told, wondering why, all of a sudden, my heart is racing as he guides me back into Walmart®.

"Do you see your mother's friend, Ms. Heath?"

"Yes. She's happy to see me and the kids, but the kids were sick from eating tacos. She watched the boys while I took Mikaylah to the bathroom."

"Then what?" Dr. Harmon asked, as he also reminded me to relax and breathe.

"After the kids got wiped off and cleaned up, Mikaylah fell asleep on the bench. Ms. Heath showed Khamm and KJ pictures of her family vacation in Wildwood and pictures of her pets and her grandkids. She's so proud of her family, and I admire pictures of her house and look at the background. I often wondered why Ms. Heath limped, but while looking at her pictures, I saw she had a prosthetic leg. That's why she limps", as I try to speak again.

BOOM!! I grab my head. This time, Dr. Harmon says, "Take a breath. Now exhale. Breathe."

My heart is racing. I feel like my heart is coming through my chest when he asks, "Do you see another picture?"

"Yes. It's her 60th birthday pictures!!"

"Look closer, Sweeah. What's on the picture?"

"I don't know. A restaurant. It's a fancy restaurant. Her family and… and…"

"Look closer, Sweeah. Do you recognize anybody else in the photos?"

Sweeah's mind races as she remembers all the photos in her head.

"MOOK!" Sweeah's voice is stuttering as she repeats the name. "Mook! Mook!" And then screams, "NO! NO! NO!" BOOM!!! She grabs her head in pain as she screams his name, "KYLE!! NO!!! NO!!!"

She opens her eyes as the tears stream down her cheeks. She sits in a state of shock, confused, and unable to process the words that have just come out of her mouth. She repeats them again, this time in a whisper, as she looks over at Dr. Harmon and his wife, who is fighting back her own tears.

"He was kissing her." She said as she touched her own lips, and then as reality started to set in, her pain quickly changed to anger; you could hear it in her voice; her tone now deepened.

"He was kissing her, and she was wearing my clothes." Sweeah closes her eyes again as if she's visualizing the pictures right now."

"He wasn't there at first. It was just Mook. I was looking for Chase, but the next pictures… Kyle…

Kyle… he's in the next picture. They are on a date, and the bitch is wearing my clothes. I was in Disney®, and he was home dicking down my best friend."

Dr. Harmon briefly looks over at his wife in awe as Sweeah laughs and sits on the edge of the chaise chair – her mind racing. She's just shaking her head in disbelief. Dr. Monica motions for her husband to remain silent. She senses that Sweeah needs this moment to allow all her inner feelings to manifest into clear visions. Visions that she can acknowledge and finally accept as hard-core facts. The ugly truth about Kyle and Mook has finally been exposed.

The air was once again 'eerie'. You could now hear a mouse piss on cotton; it was so quiet. Sweeah is mumbling something neither doctor could hear clearly. But then they both were able to hear her clear the next time. She yells in a raging fit… "The baby! She lost my husband's baby!!"

"How could they do this to me?" she said, wiping more tears from her face as she clutched the weighted blanket. And then it was like looking Satan in his face. You could see the rage in her eyes as she stood to her feet and said, "That bitch lost her baby, but they made me lose my KJ! My baby!!!"

Chapter 8

WHO ELSE KNOWS?

As if finally finding out after months of searching for answers and beating herself up wasn't enough, Sweeah had no idea that this hypnotherapy session had not only uncovered why she was driving so recklessly after leaving Walmart®, it seems as though she also unlocked parts of her childhood memory that are not written in her diary. She's saying so much while she's in her hypnotic state that once the therapist awakens her, she can't help but wonder why they were looking at her in such disbelief. After she semi-calms down, Dr. Harmon decides to expose all the information.

(Brace yourself…not even Sweeah was ready for the impact of all the gut punches coming her way.)

"Sweeah," he says gently. "You know everything you say here is confidential, right?"

"Yes," she replies, looking anxiously and confused. "Why, Dr. Harmon? What's up? Did I remember something else about Kyle? What else has he done? What else did I say?"

"Sweeah, let me be clear," he says as he glances over

at his wife again. "Yes, you mumbled a few things about Kyle, but the worst about Kyle has been exposed. Sweeah, listen. You spoke about two things that I definitely wasn't expecting to hear, and honestly, I'm not even sure if it will make sense to you!"

(Soon, Sweeah will start to piece together another family secret that nearly causes her a mental breakdown.)

"Dr. Monica, what is he talking about? What else did I say during hypnosis? What two things, Doc?"

"What else do you remember, Sweeah?" Dr. Harmon says in a low tone.

"Dr. Harmon," Sweeah says now while clinching her teeth and clapping her hands with each word… "NO DISRESPECT, BUT PLEASE GET TO THE MOTHERFUCKING POINT! I thought my husband fucking and getting my best friend pregnant was the icing on the cake, but if it's more shit, just give it all to me. Stop asking me what I remember and just fucking TELL ME… Please!!"

"Fine. Fine," he says. Dr. Monica nods her head like, 'Fuck it… give it to her straight."

"Sweeah, I'll give it to you straight, but let's be clear… this is MY office, and I have my own methods of handling medical decisions. You DO NOT dictate how I…"

"I'm sorry… I'm sorry…." Sweeah says, cutting him off. "I apologize… I'm sorry… I've been waiting months to find out what made me so enraged that I ultimately killed my precious KJ, and now, to hear that I also exposed some other inner issues, I just need to know everything now. Please!"

"Okay. You said two things crystal clear—#1. You were a small child, maybe seven years old, when you heard arguing coming from the family kitchen. Curious, you peek into the door and see your mom, your dad, Ms. Carla, and Mr. Amin arguing, so you step back but continue to listen."

"Okay, doc, that's it? That's not news. Lonna and Shae' must've done something."

"Sweeah, did you hear me say you were SEVEN years old? Lonna and Shae' were kids themselves and definitely NOT in a relationship at that young age."

I pause as I try to think back to the day he's talking about, but I can't, so I get right to the point. "What the fuck did I say, Dr. Harmon? Please go on."

"They were arguing about an orgy."

"A what?" I said, looking lost.

"An orgy!!!! Today, it would be called a swingers' party. You got very upset by the things you were hearing. The seven-year-old, you repeated things under hypnosis, but I couldn't quite make out everything you were saying, so I bent down to see if I could hear you clearer. When you paused…then Sweeah… then…"

"Go on, Dr. Harmon. PLEASE!"

"Then you – you – you had another breakthrough! It nearly made my heart stop!!"

How he was sitting up on the edge of the chair troubled me. And once he reached for my hands, he made me nervous. I knew he was definitely trying his best to find the right words when I calmly said, "Just say it…"

Dr. Monica looks at her husband and shrugs her shoulders. She then looks over at me and nods her head as if to say, 'Here's go, nothing!' I almost felt bad because I know Dr. Monica damn sure wasn't expecting her day to take this sharp turn, but to be honest, having her in here with us, witnessing all the bullshit, and not judging me is providing me with an extra sense of security and I will definitely thank her later. Still, what was said next shook me to my core!!

The Bombshell From Hell

#2 Sweeah, do you remember EVERYTHING about your RAPE???"

"Yes," I replied quickly, snatching my hand away from his. "Why?" My heart palpitations are erratic. I feel like I may vomit.

"Sweeah, did the police ever find your rapist?"

My eyes start to fill with tears as I relive the horrific events of that night in the park and the beating he put on me, as if raping me was not enough.

"Yes, the police found him. They finally found him." I said in a whisper.

He scoots closer to me, again holding my hand, and asks, "But did the police ever arrest him, Sweeah?"

"NO!" I said as tears poured down my face. "NO! They didn't arrest him!!!" Sobbing, I yelled, "They never caught him!!!"

Gently, he asks, "So how did they find him?"

"Some people found his body and called the cops. When the cops went through his things, they found pictures of me and comments on the pictures that assured the police that he was indeed my rapist, not to mention his DNA matched my rape kit."

My adrenaline is rushing as I picture him on me in the park: the odd smell and his punches. The rage is boiling inside me. I'm mad at myself because it took me years to get over this part of my life and bury it deep within.

"Sweeah. Sweeah!"

I hear Dr. Harmon call my name again. I must've drifted into a deep thought.

"Yes, I'm sorry." And I repeat myself, "His DNA matched my rape kit, so they knew it was him."

"Sweeah. LOOK AT ME!" Dr. Harmon said to me as his eyes began to meet mine. "Do you remember how he died?"

"Yes… Shae' and I killed him!!!"

You could literally hear a pin drop. Both myself and the therapists were in shock by my emotional confession. I had honestly blocked that night out as well. This revelation was just another secret of many that Shae and I shared.

For a second, I was scared. Internally asking myself, "What the fuck did you just do, Sweeah?" But I remembered that I was protected by doctor-patient confidentiality, so I decided to let it all out. FUCK IT! I've carried this secret for way too long. I take a deep breath, close my eyes, and start to release all of what happened in detail. I never knew exactly who it was, but I always felt like it wasn't a total stranger, and boy, was I right!! NEVER TRUST A WOLF IN SHEEP'S CLOTHING!

Chapter 9

THREE HOURS IN THERAPY

S till crying, I gently splash water on my face. I wasn't prepared for all the Delta hypnosis revealed today. I had buried so much so deep I, myself, had honestly forgotten so many things about my past.

"It's okay, Sweeah." Dr. Monica says as she passes me a towel to dry my face.

"Dr. Monica, I truly appreciate what you did for me today. You never left my side."

"Sweeah, I believe that God doesn't make mistakes. Not too much happens by coincidence. So, for whatever reason, I bumped into you earlier, and God laid it on my heart to stay, not just for you, but clearly, my husband needed some reinforcements, and clearly, God knew that too." Turning towards me and looking directly at me, she said, "Today was really heavy, Sweeah. Real heavy. Kyle, Lisa (Mook) – I have no clue what secrets live inside your family's kitchen, and everything you just told us about your rapist, I'm not sure how you're not in the psychiatric unit. You've been through a lot, but you're a survivor!"

She hugged me and said, "When you're ready, we will dig deeper."

I can't help the tears that once again stream down my face. I take in all the scenarios that she just ran down to me. She's absolutely correct. How am I not mentally broken down? And with that thought, we hear a tap on the bathroom door.

"Everything okay in there?" asks Dr. Harmon.

"Yes, love. We'll be right out." Dr. Monica said so lovingly to Dr. Harmon.

"Sweeah, before we leave out, let me just say this. No marriage is perfect! Lord knows my husband and I have had our share of trials, but we worked to re-invent our love and bond; we reconnected, and honestly, we both matured over the years and realized our commitment was worth fighting for."

I smile. "I'm so happy for you guys! I'm thankful you two had enough chemistry and willpower to work out all of your issues. I seriously doubt you had my problems; nevertheless, I'm grateful that y'all stuck it out. Shit today would've been much different if it were only one of you." We laughed. "But honestly, Dr. Monica… Kyle is the ENEMY! He is the reason my son is dead! I will NEVER forgive him!! Kyle is THE wolf in sheep's clothing, and I'm going to handle him!!"

Dr. Monica's face was that of grave concern because

I was no longer crying. In fact, I'm actually smiling as I now allow my inner thoughts to run rampant in my mind and quickly remind myself that it wasn't just Kyle. Mook is also gonna pay for her role in killing my precious KJ.

These were my last words to myself as we all headed back to the lobby. Dr. Harmon is clearly a pinch worried about his patient. He encourages me to continue therapy twice a week, if need be; journal daily, meditate to help calm my anxiety; and most of all, seek a higher power (Jesus, etc.) and pray because there's A LOT to process besides the three bombshells I remembered earlier—Kyle & Mook's Affair, Family Orgy Conversations, and Killing My Rapist. There's also KJ's death, Mikaylah's pregnancy, and all the unanswered questions around the pregnancy to digest.

I nod my head in agreement with Dr. Harmon. At this point, I am mentally and emotionally drained, but she is beyond words as she looks past Dr. Harmon and sees Perry waiting for me in the lobby. Happy, he ignored her and trusted his own instincts, driving to KOP to escort his friend home. Sweeah was in no shape to drive alone. Nobody needed a repeat of her driving recklessly under emotional duress.

The car ride home was silent at times. Perry, breaking the ice, said, "Don't you worry. I have someone coming to tow your car back to your house."

Sweeah couldn't help but smile as she whispered, "I forgot... you have a friend for everything!"

"Yup. Yup." Perry said playfully, causing Sweeah to let out a tiny chuckle.

Chapter 10

ROAD TRIP

So many hours had gone by. Sweeah felt beyond guilty that she hadn't talked to Khamm and Mikaylah, but just as the thought crossed her mind, her phone text message went off with the caption, "They are okay." with two selfie pictures of MeMe, Khamm, and Mikaylah and her baby bump, and Amayah. This instantly put a smile on my face. My God was definitely hearing my prayers.

Wanting to ease their worries, I took a quick selfie of Perry and myself and sent it to MeMe – captioned, 'Silly Road trip Faces.'

My smile quickly faded as my face was rather blank. My mind is yet again racing; seeing my niece was unexpected. I miss her dearly, and seeing her instantly made me think of her father. I wondered if he had dropped her off at my house or did MeMe go pick her up.

"Sweeah. Sweeah!"

I shook my head and turned to Perry, who I guessed had been talking to me, but I was zoned out.

"Yes," I say in a low tone, my mind still wondering...

"What do you want to eat? He asked. "I'm starving!" he said. "All I had was breakfast and a light snack. A brother is getting HANGRY (hungry/angry)!!!""

I let out another light chuckle, and then I realized that I clearly wasn't paying attention in the car because when I finally looked out the window, I saw we were parked on South Street. Confused, I'm like, "Perry, what the hell are we doing on South Street?"

Shaking his head from side to side, with his hand raised to his chin, he says, "Pizza! A nicca wants some good, big-sliced pizza and a Pepsi – no ice!"

If you're from Philly, then you already know that besides a great cheesesteak, South Street's Lorenzo's pizzeria, whose slices are so huge, one slice can be split into three slices – no lie! And that's for sure!

We agree on the pizza. The semi-night air feels so good. It is the perfect end-of-summer weather. No longer hot and not yet cold. Just right. We fed the parking meter and began to walk towards the pizza store.

Perry says, "Remember when you were a kid, you thought South Street was THEE PLACE TO BE! It was a sign that you had reached maturity if your parents allowed you to go to South Street. It was bigger than hanging out at the Gallery®. It was where the super fly teens and young adults went to feel grown."

Perry and I both laughed because, of course, I used to hear Lonna and her friends talk about all the grown-up stores on South Street. But in my mind, I used to visualize myself and Shae' and feel like I already had one up on South Street and Lonna.

Perry said South Street is where he saw his first openly gay couple and felt like maybe one day, he would be brave enough to live his truth, just like those guys. He's living his truth, not giving a damn about people or their opinions.

With each store we passed, we had a story. Remember your herringbone chains and onyx earrings (figure 8, bamboo, horseheads, etc.), and we wore two pair of those big ass earrings, dope ropes, and Kangos.

Our laughter was cut short as the guy asked, "What can I get you two?"

"Three slices," Perry said, "To go and two Pepsis – no ice, garlic on the side, please."

"Perry. Who's the third slice for?"

He replied, "ME, BITCH!"

I grab his arm and lay my head on his shoulder as he pays for our meal. It's so crazy! Perry has gone from being my gay work husband to my security blanket, my new best friend, and my lifesaver! After leaving the store, he says, "We have enough on the meter. Let's walk over to Penn's Landing, eat, and chill for a moment."

"Sounds good to me," I said, and off we went. I held the sodas as he carried the big pizza box. We had to be careful of the cops on horseback and the poop that came from their horses. And, not to mention the damn bicyclists who have no respect for the pedestrians walking.

"Perry," I said gently as we approached the red light at the intersection, "Thank you. Thank you! Thank you!! This entire day has been somewhat of a nightmare. I want to be honest and fill you in on all the bullshit I uncovered during my hypnotherapy session, but the truth is, some things are legally excluded from sharing (the murder)."

This statement only made Perry more curious as he wondered what she could have uncovered that would involve the law. He also wondered if this was or wasn't the right time to reveal the secret he'd been carrying around for months and if she would mentally and emotionally be able to handle it. Sweeah has NO CLUE that her dear friend has his own "bombshell" to drop on her.

As the light turns green and they proceed to Penn's Landing, he says, "Sweeah, you're welcome." But, to himself, he wonders, *I have to tell her. She needs to know the truth. She deserves to know.*

Besides, Perry had a million questions that only Sweeah could answer. He decided that he wouldn't be the one who kept vital information from Sweeah. She might as well deal with all the drama at once. Whatever she uncovered during her therapy session already had her on edge. But Perry had already promised himself that he would have Sweeah's back and protect her at any cost. See, although Perry was gay, he was also about his hands. Don't get it fucked up; he would go from lip gloss to gloves about the ones he loved. Perry knew that Sweeah needed this information to help connect all the dots and help her restore all of her memories that disappeared after the car accident.

Chapter 11

SHE DOESN'T KNOW WHAT PERRY KNOWS

" "Damn, this pizza is so good!" Sweeah said as she devoured her slice.

"Slow the hell down," Perry yelled, "You're going to choke!" They both laughed. "It's not your last supper," Perry said while still shaking his head.

The breeze from the water felt so good, the night air was crisp, and the Ben Franklin Bridge lights helped illuminate the night sky.

"So, how'd the session go?" Perry asked, breaking the awkward silence.

Shaking her head and wiping her mouth, Sweeah gently said, "I don't know."

Confused at her statement, Perry repeated the question, this time making direct eye contact. "Sweeah, HOW DID YOUR SESSION GO?"

Perry had never seen so much hurt in her eyes, and with her first blink, the tears fell and never stopped.

"EVERYTHING WAS A LIE!!" Sweeah screamed. "It was all a lie. How could he do this to me, to his kids? He lied to me, and he killed my KJ!! These were her last words as she slid down Perry's body.

Perry tried his best to hold her up, but at this point, his friend was a fucking wreck, so he slid down to the ground and rocked her slowly, and hugged her extra tight.

"Sweeah, life ain't perfect, and we all have to go through some unfair shit in life! But now ain't the time to fall the fuck apart! "GET UP!" Perry loosened his grip and extended his hand to Sweeah as he stood up.

"GET UP!!" His voice was now stern, and Sweeah knew that something was off. She wiped her eyes as she stood to her feet. Grabbing both of her hands, Perry kept the stern tone as he said, "You know I fucking love you, right? You know that my loyalty is to you."

"Perry, what is it? Just tell me! Yes, I know you love me, and …"

"I know, you're being BLACKMAILED," he blurted out.

"What??!!" Sweeah's eyes got big, and she was confused.

"Perry, I know Kyle was sleeping with Mook. I know." Fighting back all her tears, she continued to tell Perry all the devastating details she had uncovered during therapy.

"Wait!" Perry interrupted, "What do you mean sleeping with Mook?"

"Isn't that what you meant when you said Kyle was blackmailing me?"

"NO!" Perry screamed, rubbing his head and cradling his face. "I never said Kyle. Hold up! Sweeah, sit down. That's not what I meant at all. I've been keeping some information from you. I had to protect you mentally. But now I'm beyond confused."

"Wait… Blackmail?" It was as if Sweeah had a delayed reaction. "Give it to me straight, Perry! NOW!"

Sweeah's sadness was now turning to rage, and Perry knew she needed to process all of this bullshit at one time. *(Brace yourself, readers).*

There was a lot of confusion going on. "I had all of your belongings, all your work shit. I packed your desk and all the shit in your car, including all of the stuff that fell out of your pocketbook the day of the 18-wheeler accident. I thought it was a music CD, but when I put it inside my laptop, BABY! I saw you and your brother-in-law, Shae! Fornicating in every God-given position known to man, in every room of a beautiful mansion. Shocked by what I witnessed on the screen, I was confused as to why y'all would tape yourselves. That's when I noticed the packaging and realized someone had mailed this to you. Now, I ain't stupid! I figured it out!"

Embarrassed and scared, Sweeah put her head down in disbelief. After 20 years, her secret was finally exposed, and her world crumbled all around her. The silence seemed like forever until Perry said, "Bitch, that's fucked up! But that's your business, not mine. Who am I to judge?"

Taking in all those words, Sweeah fell into Perry's arms, screaming, "Why me?! What's happening to my life? What have I done? I'm losing everything, Perry. I'm losing everything!!"

Crouching down to the ground again, he says, "GET UP AND GET A GRIP!!" with a straight, stern face. "How long?"

Sweeah wasn't sure if she had heard him right, so through her snot and tears, she repeated his statement, "How long?"

"Yes, Sweeah. Just how long have you been fucking your sister's husband? And Sweeah, I swear to God, you better tell me the truth, the whole truth and nothing but the truth, so help me Gawd! I got you, but not if you lie!!"

At that point, Sweeah knew that Perry was her only out. She extended her hand to him and asked him to sit beside her. As he obliged, she pulled out her cell phone, wiping away the river of tears, and said, "Hey MeMe, listen. Perry and I are a bit tied up, so can you stay the night? I'll be there; I'm just not sure what time. Okay. Thanks. Love you too." What Perry heard as Sweeah put her phone away had him baffled.

"Twenty years," she whispered as she wiped her face on the sleeve of her shirt.

Perry's face is priceless, and he's speechless as Sweeah repeats the statement, "Twenty fucking years!"

As these words leave Sweeah's lips, she feels horrified, yet a sense of relief, like a 50 lb. weight has just been lifted off her shoulders. This secret has kept her in a mental prison, but now she has no choice but to come clean, and she's ready.

"Sweeah, what the hell do you mean 20 years? And, baby, if my math is correct, that would mean you were only about 12 years old! So, did you mean two years?"

"No, Perry. Twenty-plus years, and before I lose my nerve, let me get it all off my chest. I was 12 years old; he was 17. I was 12 years old when he lured me and orally seduced me. I was 12 years old, running, playing, just being a kid – wild and free. I was 12 years old when I asked myself, *why me?*"

"That nigga raped you?" Perry asked while jumping to his feet.

Still sitting and speaking in a low tone, I replied, "NO! NEVER!! He wasn't the one who raped me."

Perry is now in way too deep after hearing her last statement. He says, "Sweeah, wait... you were raped?"

Nodding her head, "Yes. Brutally raped and left in the

dirt and bush like a dog to die."

At this point, Perry is more focused on the vicious rape than the adulterous situation with her brother-in-law. "When?"

Ignoring his question, she zones out and asks, "How did Delta miss the blackmail?" while looking into the empty sky.

"Who is Delta?" Perry asked in a softer tone.

After explaining "what" not "who" Delta was, Perry now wished that she had uncovered all the demons hidden in her mind while under hypnosis.

"Sweeah, listen. I'm not sure why this information didn't surface in your mind during that deep Delta session, but the fact still remains that besides me, you, and Shae, somebody else not only knows but has hard-core proof of that affair, and let me say that the DVD, that jawn is clear and very detailed, very physical, very intense."

"Yes, Perry, I get it. Just how much of it did you watch? Damn!" And in that not-so-funny moment, they both let out a little chuckle.

"Well, shit, Sweeah, I had to be sure I wasn't seeing things. Shit, that strong back, mocha muthafucker, all long donging you from all angles, dicking you down…"

"Perry! Stop it!!" Sweeah says while hitting his arm.

"Okay. Okay! My bad!! Shae's fine ass got you in all kinds of bullshit…"

Breaking the awkward silence, Perry says, "Bitch, we need a plan."

"What kind of plan?" Sweeah asks. "I'm literally still processing all the shit I've learned today. So, let's run down that list of mental torture. My husband is fucking my best friend, and if she hadn't lost the baby, how was she gonna explain that? Who was she gonna blame the baby on?"

"WAIT!!! Hold the fuck up! Pregnant? Wait…" At this point, Perry was having a gay-pride hissy fit. With his hand waving in all directions, he repeats himself again and again. "The devil is a liar! Pregnant?!"

"Yes, Perry. Mook's ass was pregnant by my soon-to-be ex-husband. I was so busy fucking my sister's husband I didn't notice that my best friend was fucking mine."

"Bitch, you need to write a book. This shit is a bestseller!"

"Perry!!"

"No, Sweeah! You got me so fucked up in the head right now; I'm just trying my best to keep up."

"Well, Perry. That makes two of us. I had no idea that TODAY I would learn the hard truth about karma. You do dirt, you get dirt, right?"

"Yeah, but fuck that!" Perry said. "We're not having no pity party right now. We need to find out who else knows about you and Shae'. And how long have they known? If they sent you that DVD, then they want you to know that your secret is out! It was taped in the Disney® Mansion. So, who all knew you were going there?"

"Nobody, Perry. We were sneaking, remember?"

"Ok. Ok. Girl, I gotta call my detective friend…"

"No, you will NOT! I can't involve others. It's bad enough, you know. I trust you! We'll have to figure this out on our own, Perry! Please?"

"Okay. Okay. I got you."

After a moment, Perry says, "20 years, bitch? Damn. I'm jealous!"

"You're sick, Perry."

"You have some nerve, Mrs. Evans/Evans. Damn, even after you divorce Kyle, your name is still going to be Sweeah Evans."

"It's all good, Perry. I might change it. And Perry…"

"Yes, Sweeah?"

"Years ago, I was headed home during a football pep rally. I was just a kid. That's the answer to your "When?" question.

Perry looked at Sweeah and nodded his head without saying another word about it.

It was at that point my cell phone rang. "Hey, MeMe. Yes, we're okay. Just catching up on a few things…"

Perry grabs the phone and interjects, "We're on our

way now, MeMe. Sorry we took so long. It's been a while since we spent some quality time together."

"No worries, Perry," MeMe says. "Take y'all time. Everyone in here is sleeping."

"Okay, Mom. Love you."

"Love you too."

The phone hangs up, and Perry suggests that it's getting late and we should head home. The walk back from Penn's Landing to the car was emotional. Perry and I both were mentally and emotionally drained. We walked hand in hand, my head resting on her shoulder, and at that moment, he squeezed my hand, letting me know that he had my back no matter what.

No words were spoken.

Chapter 12

WHAT'S THE PLAN?

As the sun comes up, I'm still stuck in bed. I was up all night, tossing and turning. How did I get here? This was my last thought before there was a knock on my bedroom door.

Knock-knock.

"Mom, you woke?"

"Yes, Mik. Come in. You, okay?"

"Yeah. These kicks are beyond intense."

We laughed as I rubbed her belly and said good morning to my grandson. Not even three minutes had gone by before Khamm came jumping onto my bed.

"Good morning, Mommy! I'm hungry!! MeMe said she's tired and you should cook."

Mikaylah laughed. "I'm hungry too!"

I knew I had no energy to stand up and cook, so I yelled, "Everybody get dressed! We're going out for breakfast!!"

"YAY!" the kids said as they both ran out of my room. I finally got up and headed to the shower. I can hear

MeMe saying she wanted chicken and waffles. I laugh as I turn on the shower. I caught a flashing light out of my peripheral view on the nightstand. My cell phone is buzzing. My ringer is off. I quickly pick up my phone when I see the name, Dr. Monica.

"Hello?"

"Hello, Sweeah. It's Dr. Monica. I hope it's not a bad time…"

"No, Dr. Monica. It's fine. Is everything okay?"

"Yes, sweetheart. I'm just checking on you. Yesterday's session was beyond intense, and with all you uncovered, I just wanted to check on you."

"Thank you. That means a lot to me, but I'm okay. I met with a friend after my session, and I was able to vent in a safe space and release a lot of that pent-up aggravation and try to figure out what I need to do next in my life."

"Okay, Sweeah. I hear you. Just be mindful that all actions have consequences, so moving forward, make good decisions, and remember, it's not just you. You have two beautiful children and a grandbaby on the way. Sometimes, it's okay not to have a comeback or get somebody back. Understand?

"Yes, doctor. I understand and thank you."

"Mom? Are you ready?"

"One second, Khamm. Mommy is on the phone."

"Oh, I'm sorry," Dr. Monica said, "I'll let you go."

"Thanks, Doctor. Family breakfast is at a restaurant today, not here in the kitchen."

We both laugh and hang up after saying goodbye.

After jumping in the shower and throwing on a sweatsuit, we all headed out the door. MeMe catches me as I stop midstride. The picture of KJ hanging on the wall catches my attention. She stroked my back and said, "Let's go to his favorite place." I smiled, thinking about him ordering pancakes with crispy edges. I touched his photo and replied, "Yes. Let's do that." It was at this point that I decided I had to avenge his death by any means necessary.

I should've listened to Dr. Monica! Revenge isn't always needed. Just wait for KARMA!

****

It's been a few days since shit hit the fan, and all my secrets were exposed. I felt like shit, so I called Bianca to see if I could get my hair done. Everyone is still overextending themselves after KJ's death, so she graciously squeezed me in.

Once I left the hair salon, I went back home to change my clothes. I really wished I had just stayed outside. As I pulled up to the house, I saw Kyle's car. My anxiety hit the roof. What the fuck is he doing here? This nigga has the balls to show his face at my house! I swung the door open, ready to snap, when MeMe walked towards me, shaking her head from side to side, like "No. No. Not right now."

"Mom! Look what Dad brought me!" Khamm said. I had to fake a smile for my baby's sake, as MeMe said, "Grin and bear it. It's not about you. It's about Khamm."

"Oh baby, that's so nice," I said, looking at the huge remote-control truck. If looks could kill, Kyle would be six feet under, and so would I because the look he gave me was complex. His first look said *damn, she looks good, fresh from the salo*n. Then the look shifted to *that bitch killed my son!*

Feeling the tension in the air, Mikaylah said, "Let's take the truck outside, fellas. Come on, let's see what all it can do, Khamm."

Beyond excited, Khamm screams, "Dad! Come on! Let's go!!" pulling his hand and jumping up and down as all three head outside.

"Dammit, Sweeah, you said you'd be a while. So, when Kyle called asking about Khamm, I said okay, come over."

"It's okay, MeMe. Kyle is my problem, NOT yours. Not the kids. All mine!" See, at this point, MeMe only knows that Kyle blames me for KJ's death. She has no clue about Kyle and Mook, and what I saw that day in Ms. Heath's pictures at Walmart are the reasons I left the store beyond distraught, but it's okay.

"Mom, I'm going upstairs to change my clothes. Can you please convince him to leave soon?"

The look MeMe gave me was like, *I'm fed up with everybody except the kids.*

I sat in silence for a quick second again, reflecting on how the hell I got here. I think about the pros and cons.

PROS	CONS
My grandson is on the way	My KJ is dead
2 of my kids survived	My secret is out about Shae
My job is still available	I'm being blackmailed
Friends and family still support me & don't blame me at all	I'm getting divorced
I didn't have a mental breakdown after Delta Hypnosis and Perry's confession	My bestie and husband are now my enemies
Did I mention that I wasn't the one who was pregnant? Thank God!	Therapy uncovered too many buried tragedies
Perry has my back	My kid's entire lifestyle has changed.

I have a baby shower to plan	I'm now a single mom.
I'm in counseling, which is good and bad	I'm too busy dealing with all my own shit. I'm not supporting Mikaylah, Khamm, or even MeMe, who did lose her grandson

All these thoughts creep into my mind, but in this next moment, I cracked somewhat of a smile as I quickly thought about, in a few months, I'm going to be a damn grandmom. I smile even more, thinking back to my own pregnancies. Then, on queue, here comes Satan, making me think back to Shae and how he literally took the role of God Dad to the extreme. He loves kids, and at that time, he and Lonna didn't have any children yet.

"Girl, get out of your head," is what I told myself as I went to my closet to look for another outfit to wear. Looking into the mirror, I instantly felt great.

"Oh, Mom, you look gorgeous!" Mikayla said as she stood in my doorway.

"Thanks, baby," I said with an air kiss.

"Is he…?"

"Yes, Mom, he's gone."

"I hate that he blames you for KJ dying. It was an accident, Mom."

"I know, sweetheart, but it's okay. I know what really happened. We know it was an accident. All things will come to light soon, but for now, let's focus on all things positive."

"Good, because…," Mikaylah hesitates, "I wanted to know if we could switch my room to the boys' room? But if it's too much to ask, I'll understand."

Silence fills the room…

"No, it's fine. I know you'll need more space and…" *(a few tears)* Sweeah opens her arms.

"Mom. Nevermind. I'm sorry. I shouldn't have asked. I'm sorry."

"No, Mikaylah, it's time! It's time to gather KJ's things and move forward. We'll make it a fun day. A packing party! I'll need lots of wine." We both laugh as I hug her tight. "I love you, Mikaylah. And I guess, the sooner, the better."

She breaks free from my embrace as she runs to tell her grandmother that I said yes. I could hear the cheers all the way upstairs. At this point, I go stand in the doorway of Mik's room, then walk over to the boy's room. So many emotions, so many memories of KJ and Khamm in here… And just when I was in a positive space, I look over at the vent on the floor. I walk over to it and kneel down and remove the grate cover and stupidly scoop up that damn diary. *Why Sweeah? Why??!!*

Chapter 13

SO THAT'S WHO THEY ARE! IDENTITIES EXPOSED.

Dear Diary:
Shae' is going to college next week. I'm kind of sad. I'm having so many mixed emotions. What if he gets into an out-of-state college? Why can't he just go to community college? Is it selfish of me to pray the opposite of everyone else's prayers?

Dear God:
It's me, Sweeah. Please DO NOT give Shae' that football scholarship. Let him go to one of our local colleges, Temple, LaSalle, Drexel, or even Villanova... No, that's too far. God, just keep him close to home. Amen.

Quickly, I shut the diary as I heard Mikaylah yelling my name. "Mom! Perry is here!

"Girl, I hope you're dressed. I'm coming up. Who cares if you're dressed or not!" he said, "I have news..."

Quickly, I jump up to hide the diary and stash it.

Just because Perry now knows about me and Shae', I don't need him wanting to read the details. As he entered the room, he quickly shut my room door.

"Sweeah!! Bitch!! I got news!!!"

The look on his face and the rolling of his eyes, mixed with the smacking of the lips, warned me that this was going to be juicy.

"Perry, what the hell happened?" He dramatically put up his two fingers.

"First thing... Remember when you were having bad headaches, and MeMe took you to the ER, and you were treated by that doctor that also treated Lonna's eye in Disney?"

"Yes." I say, extra curious, "Go on!!"

"Well, Bitch! I had the good doctor followed, and now you need to help me to connect these dots."

"Wait nigga... What do you mean followed?"

"Sweeah..." he said while pacing around the room, looking confused but smelling so damn good as usual. "Sweeah, you be dragging shit out. So, I hired my PI to investigate him. Shit, like you said, what were the odds of good ole Dr. Pitts treating two sisters in two different states?"

I knew Perry all too well, so I knew he was trying to spill some real tea.

"Perry! Dammit!!! What is it?"

"Okay! Okay, Bitch! Calm down," he said as he pulled a manila envelope from his jacket. "My PI snapped these pictures of him on separate days, but on four days, he's with two of the same women. They look familiar, but I wasn't sure who they were, so I had my guy investigate them."

Snatching the envelope, Sweeah nearly passed out as she looked at the two ladies in the photos, wondering what the fuck was going on. Lonna's two friends from Disney, Stix, and Yasmine, are in the photos with Dr. Pitts. Perry couldn't contain himself.

"Bitch! Brace yourself! They are his sisters!!"

"Wait? What? His sisters? Are you sure?"

"Sweeah, don't play with me! I only come correct." Perry said, rolling his eyes.

"What the fuck is going on, Perry?"

"I don't know, but it seems like little Miss Lonna got some skeletons busting out her closet."

"Yeah, I knew those two chicks weren't childhood friends, and she didn't randomly bump into them in Disney. And what were the odds that Dr. Pitts not only treated her, but they acted like they didn't already know each other?"

"Perry! OH SHIT!!! I just remembered something!"

"What, Sweeah? Bitch, spill it!"

"So, for a while, I was thinking maybe Lonna was gay because Yasmine is a soft butch, but now I'm thinking she's fucking around with the doctor because a few months ago, remember Bianca told me Lonna had an abortion and was asking me how she was doing, so I just played along, but Shae' would never go for her getting an abortion."

"Yeah, why would you want to abort your husband's child?"

"Exactly! Unless it wasn't your husband's."

"Girlllll......" Perry said as he started fake slapping my back. "The drama!!! Bitch, we have a mystery to solve!"

As I stand up with these photos in my hand, I say to Perry, "In due time, everything will come to a head."

I just didn't know that all hell was about to break loose. I was so fixed on Lonna and Dr. Pitts, Stix, and Yasmine that I forgot to ask Perry about the second thing his PI investigated. But Perry didn't. Before he left, he gave MeMe another sealed envelope and asked her to give it to me before bed.

Mentally, bracing myself for what was in the second envelope is what I thought I had done, but I had mixed feelings as I read the pages. I sat back on my bed and reread the information.

Name: Hondo Miguel Guzman (Miguel)
Age: 17

Race: Mexican-American
Height: 5'10"
Weight: 180
Residence: Miami, FL
High School, etc., were all included.

Perry had also investigated who Mikaylah's baby daddy was. There wasn't a lot of information, but it was a start and way more than I had. It was time to talk to Mikaylah; the baby would be here soon. I need to know what I'm really dealing with.

I call Perry. He picks up, saying, "What, Sweeah?"

"Really, midget?" We both laugh. As I say, "How? No, why did you leave me alone with that new information?"

"I figured you might want to process all of that alone. I dropped two bombs on you in one night. Besides, I had a date, girl! But it's over. That's tomorrow's gossip. Let's get into this new son-in-law of yours.

We both laugh as Sweeah says, "Well, it's not too much info, and what's here isn't bad. He graduated high school, which is a bonus, thank God. At least the baby's parents will be educated. Mikaylah's school was gracious enough to let her homeschool after the accident, and she passed everything.

"Sweeah, it's weird. My guy could only find out those things, but the most important thing was that he had no criminal record and got good grades in school. He played a few sports, but he's been good so far. You want him to keep digging?"

"No, it's time for me to talk to Mikaylah. But thank you, Perry. For everything!"

"No worries, Sweeah. I got you!"

Falling asleep is now impossible. This month has been so unpredictable. With all the family discoveries during hypnosis to now finding out Dr. Pitt is related to Lonna's friends to finally having the name of Mikaylah's baby daddy and a clear picture of him, I know Perry stole it off Mikaylah's social media. He's really handsome, meaning my grandson could come out looking like an Indian from my side, Mexican, or honestly like neither. It doesn't matter as long as he's healthy. These are my thoughts as I drift off. I guess my body was exhausted.

Chapter 14

THE SHADE

Morning came, and I honestly don't remember falling asleep. I lay in bed again, recapping the events of this month. I said my morning prayers, and before I could say Amen, the devil had already attacked me.

The house was quiet, but as I lay still in bed, the faint sound of laughter made me sit up. The voices were familiar, but I couldn't quite make out who it was, so I got out of bed, washed my face, brushed my teeth, combed my hair down, threw on my comfy Crocs® and headed down the hall towards the steps, when I heard the voice say clear as day, "Thank you for making me a part of planning the shower, MeMe. You know I'll do anything for my niecey-poo."

I couldn't get down the steps fast enough, and once I approached the group of ladies, I made straight eye contact while these words left my lips…

"Well, well, well…if it ain't Aunt Mook! Long time no see…Where have you been hiding?"

"Hey, Sweeah. I know, I'm sorry. So much has been going on. I just got caught up."

"Really?" I said, "Caught up?"

And before I could finish my damn sentence, here comes MeMe out of the kitchen, "Well, good, almost afternoon, Sweeah! We are just about to finalize roles and responsibilities for the shower. You've been through so much. We want you to take care of Mikaylah for that day."

My blood was boiling. This is my first time seeing Mook since I've been up and out of the hospital. I want to punch her dead in her mouth, but I have to remember *NOBODY* here knows she's fucking Mikaylah's dad, so for now I have to be calm. But mark my word, Mook *AND* Kyle are gonna regret this *backstabbing bullshit*. And yes, I have some nerve after all. I'm throwing stones, and I live in a glass house.

I'm glad MeMe's shower meeting was almost over because the tension between Mook and me was becoming too much. She barely looked at me. She received a fake phone call and said to MeMe that unfortunately she had to go, but she had the decorations and Mikaylah's outfit for the day.

"Aunt Mook?"

"Yes, Mik?"

"Look at the picture I just sent to your phone. That's the dress I really like."

"Okay. Got it. I love it!" Mook said while giving Mikaylah a hug goodbye and air kisses to the other baby shower members.

They all thought I was crazy as I busted out laughing. The thought of me fucking Mook up gave me internal pleasure.

"Sweeah, you okay over there?"

"Oh, yes, MeMe. Just thinking how nice this shower is gonna be, right Mikaylah?"

"Right, Mom. But what if the weather is bad on that day?" Mikaylah's face was fearful.

"Well, Mikaylah, that's a chance we have to take. You're due in February, so the shower has to be in January. People come out in the cold, honey. Don't worry." These are the comments from MeMe's church friends. These girls can cook. This is why it's a must that they cook the food for the baby shower.

As the day went on and the house was cleared out, I asked MeMe how Mook got the decorator role. Confused, MeMe said, "Sweeah, did you forget your best friend does interior design? Decorating is one of her hobbies. What's going on? You two need to fix whatever has y'all at odds. I'm tired of all this tension. Does Mook blame you for KJ? Is that the problem?"

No MeMe. She's fucking Kyle. They've been having an affair for months. That's what I found out at Walmart. That's why I was driving so recklessly that day. I saw her and Kyle out to dinner, kissing, and the bitch had on my fucking clothes!

Silence filled the air as I heard Meme saying, "Sweeah, snap out of it! Do you hear me talking to you?" I shook my head and blinked, wishing I could've really said that to Momma Evans.

"No. I don't know if she blames me, Mom, and honestly, I don't care if she does..." is the last thing I said as I stormed off.

I couldn't get my phone out fast enough. "Perry! You're not gonna believe who was just in my damn house!!"

"Who, girl? Who?!" Perry shouted.

"Fucking Mook!"

"What??!! Mook? For real? Why?"

I woke up to a house full of baby shower planners. And MeMe asked her to do all the decorations, etc."

"Well, she is good at that, Sweeah."

"Perry!!"

"What? She is!"

Just as I'm about to go deep into this ratchet conversation, my other line clicks. It's Ms. Carla.

"Perry, I'll call you back," I said, still pissed.

"Hey, Ms. Carla."

"How's all my girls doing?" she asked in her sweetest voice. "And how's my great God grandson?" she said so proudly.

"We are doing good, and he is getting so big, kicking his mommy's butt in that belly. Non-stop kicks now," Sweeah said as they both laughed.

"Sweeah, can you come by? I bought so much stuff. I want you to take a look at it. I asked MeMe this morning on the phone during the shower meeting. Should I have Amin assemble this stuff or leave it in the boxes?"

"Ms. Carla, how much did you buy?" I said as I grabbed my forehead. "Okay. Okay. Let me jump in the shower and get dressed. I'll come over."

"Okay," She said. "Come alone. I don't want Mikaylah to see any of this stuff until the baby shower."

"Okay. No problem. Give me 45 minutes."

"Okay, baby. See you soon," she said.

Chapter 15

SORRY! NOT SORRY!

I call Perry back as I head over to Ms. Carla's house. Did this fool not answer my call and instead send me an audio text?

"Girl, it's him! The liar from last night! Give me 15 minutes. He's trying to explain the unexplainable. LOL!"

I reply, "Okay. Call me back, fool."

As I sit at a red light, I smile, thinking about how, despite all the negative nonsense, Mik's shower is gonna be amazing. It's a good thing we are gonna switch bedrooms. This baby is going to have too much shit. Ms. Carla must have heard me pull up and close my car door, because she's outside her front door with open arms.

"Hello, Sweeah," she whispered in my ears as she embraced me oh so tightly. "Come on in."

I couldn't believe how much baby stuff was in her living room. My mouth fell open.

"Ms. Carla! What the hell is all of this?" I was literally in shock looking at the infant overhaul. Tears filled my eyes. It was like Mikaylah already had a baby shower.

"Oh, Sweeah, stop it! It's my first great-God grandbaby so that I may have gone overboard."

Alright, listen up. You read this right. Shae' is the God dad. Mikaylah is Ms. Carla's God granddaughter. So, the baby is her great-God grandson. LOL!!!

"You think?" I said, still in disbelief. I slowly walk over to different bags and boxes and look at stuffed animals, a swing, a bassinet, clothes, a potty, etc.

"Ms. Carla, did you leave anything on the registry?" I said as I wiped my eyes.

"Well, listen. I figured that the baby is going to be here at times, and he'll have all that he needs. I'm sure she will get double of everything, which is good, it can go to your mom's house or Mook's.

And just like that, the tears dried up, and I said with a smile, "No, he won't be going to Mook's house. She laughed, saying, Oh, okay. I agree. Mook has no baby experience." I just grinned and shook my head like if you only knew the other reason.

Ms. Carla came towards me and said, "Everything happens for a reason." She rubbed my back and said, "Uncle KJ is smiling down on us." I laughed and cried at the same time, hearing the words, 'Uncle KJ.' I felt like falling to the floor, but I'm learning to keep it together. The phone rings, breaking the sad moment.

"You need a ride now? I thought you said at least

another hour, Amin. Okay, okay. I'm on my way."

I was confused because the front door opened as she was saying Mr. Amin's name on the phone. I thought it was him, but Lord, have mercy, it was Shae'!

Now, remember I haven't seen anybody since I first left the hospital. I guess people gave me my space after I learned that KJ died.

"Hey, son. How are you? What brings you by today?" she said as she hugged him tightly.

"Hey Mom!" he said as he hugged her back, while looking at me over her shoulder.

Instantly, I licked my lips, and he smiled, looking at me so seductively.

"Where's Dad?" he asked. "I was gonna see if he wanted to go shoot some pool."

"Oh baby, he's not here. He had an appointment. I'm on my way to pick him up now. I will be a while, but you can wait if you want. If not, lock up after yourself."

"Okay, Mom. I think I'll stick around and catch up with Ms. Evans here."

I looked at him, then hugged Ms. Carla and thanked her again as she headed out the door. She turned around and said, "Oh, I forgot. Shae' is half responsible for all this baby stuff, too. So, fuss him out as well! BYE!"

But once the door was shut, neither of us was thinking about baby items.

"Hey," he said softly."

"Hey, you," I replied.

"How are you holding up?" he asked. "It's been a while since I last saw you."

The crazy thing is, the last time he saw me, I was freshly wounded. But right now, I'm freshly showered.

"I'm doing good," I said with a smile.

"Well, you damn sure look amazing."

"Really?" I said, tossing my hair back.

We both laughed, but then there was silence.

"Well, I should be going," I said, reaching for my purse on the couch.

Leaping forward, he grabbed my bag and said, "What's the rush? You just got here."

"No," I said, still semi-laughing, "You just got here." I tried my best not to make eye contact. Bad enough, his fucking hand was on mine as he moved my purse away from me. I shake my head as I try not to acknowledge that he's pulling me closer, wrapping his arms around me. I can't help but inhale his cologne's aroma. My hands, which were once by my side, are now stroking his back as he hugs me oh so tight but still gentle.

With each sensual squeeze, he pulls me in more and more, my face now up against his chest, his chin on top of my head; he's gently hugging me, moving side to side. No words for what seemed like forever.

For the first time in months, I felt so damn safe. So, loved. So, understood. And in the next breath, he said, "I'm here, Sweeah. I got you! It's okay to let it out!"

Damn. Damn! DAMN!!

And in that very moment, I felt so reconnected. Call me crazy, but ask yourself this… does your partner know your *LOVE LANGUAGE*? As the tears fall down my face, he holds me, constantly saying, "It's okay, baby. I'm here. I won't leave you."

Flashes of KJ filled my head: his smile, his laugh, his playfulness… I can't even remember falling to the floor, but when I opened my eyes and tried to wipe my face, Shae' was already wiping my tears away. Smiling, staring me right in my face, and without warning, the kissing started. My pussy was pulsating as I lay on my back, watching him take his shirt off. My mind was trying hard to fight the urge. It's been months since we last fucked in Disney World®. I instantly have a flashback of him throwing me up against the guest house doors. And, another flashback of meeting him at the hotel. Another flashback of me fucking him all over the mansion.

As I snap out of my daze, I exhale oh so deeply as Shae's tongue has once again found its way to unlock Pandora's box. I must have erupted lava five times from my inner volcano because the taste of my cum has always driven him crazy. How we got naked in his mother's house again was beyond me. I thought about stopping for a second, but she said she'd be a while, and the feeling was unexplainable. His moans, his hands underneath my thighs pulling my pussy closer to his mouth. He was going crazy, causing multiple eruptions. Somehow, we switched positions. I'm sitting on his face backwards, facing his dick, it's 69 time, which I love. Now that I'm leaning forward, taking all his manhood in my jaws, he inserts his finger into my pussy and his tongue into my ass. "Lord Have Mercy!" This feeling is just too intense for both of us. I need him inside me. I need to be fucked and the way he was going crazy from all that head, I knew he was ready to beat my back out. So, I decided to climb on top of his dick and sit on it slowly, teasing him all the way down. See, I know it kills him when I'm in control. I know how bad he wants my pussy, so I make sure I go up and way down, then come back up before I finally sit all the way down on that pipe and go to work.

The loud moans turned me on. The shit I was saying to him made him thrust his dick inside me harder and harder. *My God! My God! My God!* It hurt so good. With every thrust, I could look at his face, the way he bit his bottom lip, the tighter he squeezed his eyes, all this meant his own volcano was about to erupt and boy oh boy did it ERUPT! The breathing slowed, and the movements stopped as he panted my name. "Sweeeeeaaaaaahhhhhh!!!"

As I lay there, slumped on his chest, he graciously ran his fingers repeatedly across my back, kissing my forehead and finally saying, "Sweeah, are you okay?"

A tear fell down my face as I think back to 20 years ago in the driveway on Church Hill when he first spoke those words and where all of this craziness first began. It was at this very moment I realized that I had once again relapsed on my drug of choice, Shae' Hughes.

Sorry! Not Sorry!

The more we fight it, the stronger the connection. The more we deny it, the more we crave it. The more we get it, the more we want it. The yearning, the chemistry, the lusting, the jealousy, the intensity, it's not overreacting, it's an OBSESSION!

And when you're obsessed, you don't think clearly. You're in the moment. Sometimes, you're acting erratic, but always remember that every action has a reaction. I had no idea things were about to get so out of control. I had no clue that my next visit to hypnosis would drop a bombshell. How did I overlook this information with all that was uncovered during Delta? It's crazy! I never thought that this new uncovered info was even a possibility.

Chapter 16

NOT, AGAIN!

As I lay in bed and watch the sun come up, I toss and turn, thinking about yesterday's encounter with Shae'. His scent, his tongue, his touch, the weight of his words when he talks that shit to me. *DAMN!* I love him. I truly missed him.

These thoughts now have my fingers inside my own pussy, but it's not enough. I reach underneath my mattress to get my problem solver. Lord knows nobody or nothing can compete with Shae', but this mini vibrator on medium is a beast!

Have you ever masturbated and the orgasm was so good, you made your own self cry? *DAMN!! DAMN!! DAMN!!*

Now that I've tired myself out, I once again lay in silence, wondering if I should tell Shae' what I had learned about Lonna and Dr. Pitt. But then I asked myself, *Sweeah, what the fuck did you actually learn except that they know each other and the girls from Disney® are his sisters?* The anger builds as it seems that Lonna has won again.

Then it hits me… Ask Shae' why he allowed Lonna to get an abortion. Was there something wrong with the baby? I'm sure this news will devastate Shae' since he couldn't have known she was pregnant. Yup! Let's see you get out of this lie, Lonna!!!

Just then, I called Dr. Monica to confirm my hypnosis appointment with her husband. I call Perry and vent.

"Hello? Good morning, Biatchhh," he said laughing.

"Wassup, new best friend?" I replied as I yelled, "Oh my God, I relapsed!!!"

"Bitchhhh, what??!! Seriously? When? How? Wait, where?"

"Don't judge me," I said as I whispered, "At Ms. Carla's house on the floor."

We both bust out laughing like we were teenagers exchanging sexy secrets. At this moment, I'm kind of happy that Perry knows everything and he doesn't judge me at all. I know I can trust him. Perry is so crazy! He wanted details, and my dumb ass gave him blow-by-blow.

"Giiirrrllll" he said, "I guess this 20-year sexcapade is the real deal. I mean it sucks that it's your brother-in-law, because the history and the chemistry is fucking amazing!"

I listen to Perry's words and reply, "Yeah, it sucks because he's my true soulmate."

Silence takes over for a moment, then Perry says,

"Well if he can't be your soul mate, keep him as your sex-mate!"

We both start laughing again as I agree again and tell Perry I have another therapy appointment and that I'll call him later.

"Do you need an escort?" he asked genuinely.

"No. I'm good. But thanks, friend."

The call ends, and I jump out of bed, get showered, and get dressed. I headed downstairs to find a letter from MeMe on the table.

> *"Hey, Sweets, the kids and I went to breakfast. I know you have an early doctor's appointment, so we won't be back anytime soon. Khamm is going out with his granddad to mini golf, and Mikaylah and I are doing last-minute baby shower errands.*
>
> *Xoxo Mom*
>
> *P.S. I put all the mail on the counter.*

Seriously… I had to stop dead in my tracks and say a special thank you prayer for my parents. Lord knows MeMe and Dad have stepped up and literally kept me from drowning in my depression. I could *NOT* have made it through losing my son, and the shit from my marriage, if they didn't step in to assist me in my everyday life.

As I said, "Amen", I went over to the counter to sort through the mail, when one envelope's bright color caught my attention. It's addressed to me, but there is no return address. I opened it up and nearly died as I read the few words on the postcard with the Disney® logo. "Guest House and Mansion". Just when I thought shit was finally dying down, I realized that the person who sent that DVD of me and Shae' in Disney® was still lurking around. I bit my bottom lip in anger as I ripped up the postcard. I replay what Perry told me about the DVD he watched with Shae' and me, but still, I have no clue who could be behind this bullshit, but maybe Perry's PI can help me find out.

Chapter 17

UNEXPECTED MEMORY

"Good morning, Sweeah." Dr. Monica said as I entered the office. "My husband has almost finished his last session."

"Good morning," I said. "No rush. I'll grab a seat over here."

Baffled by my nonchalant response, Dr. Monica made her way over to where I sat. "Move over," she said sternly. "What's going on? Talk to me!"

This is so weird because although Dr. Harmon, her husband, is my actual therapist, Dr. Monica and I really connected after my DELTA session. She knows everything, so I look at her and say, "Same shit, different day… then again, new SHIT today," and as soon as I start to tell her about the mail, Dr. Harmon's door opens, his patient comes out, and he motions for me to come in. I get up and tell Dr. Monica to stay close. I might need her again.

"Sweeah, come in… come in. How are you today?"

I plop down on the couch and ask, "Where should I begin?"

"That bad?" he asked.

"Honestly, Doc… I'm so confused right now. First, I'm wondering how and why negative things keep happening in my life, and honestly, if my past choices are now my present-day karma, like, "What the fuck?""

"Well…." He says as he approaches the chair closer to me, "Remember that for every action, there is a reaction. Not necessarily karma, but hey, if you have unprotected sex (action), you could make a baby (reaction), not bad karma, just life's cycle."

"Listen, let's just get into it. Let's find out why I didn't recall being blackmailed in that intense DELTA session. You definitely had a lot to unpack. Maybe today, there's more to be exposed.

Jesus, take the wheel! For I had no *damn* clue that DELTA was gonna take an unexpected plot twist. I wasn't prepared for what I uncovered. As the process begins, I feel myself start to drift off. I'm relaxed, and my mind is somewhat racing. I start to feel anxious as different thoughts run through my mind.

I'm not sure what Dr. Harmon said differently, but at this very moment, I visualize myself being back at work, freshly back from the family's Disney® vacation. Things are kind of foggy, but I remember getting a package at work. I remember the day nearly ending and me going into the conference room, putting the DVD into the player, and watching in horror as I watched Shae' and myself being recorded in all types of sexual positions in the mansion in Disney World®.

I faintly hear Dr. Harmon saying, "It's okay, Sweeah. It's okay. Calm down."

I'm now crying as I recall the fear I felt that day in the office at work. The fear of not only being secretly recorded but who the fuck knows that I'm from Philly and also knows where I work. Who would benefit from doing this shit to me? And why wait months to open up these old wounds? Clearly, they knew me, so they know I just lost my son – and still, they don't care about fucking with my mind?!

This memory was one I expected. The next one came out of the blue again!

"Sweeah, let's go back to your childhood. Was it a good childhood? Were you happy? When, if at any time, did you feel afraid? Who was the disciplinarian in your house?"

I answered all the questions, but I get very upset at this one memory. I can recall being scolded by my Dad as a child. This stuck out because Dad was always the pushover parent. MeMe was the one we knew not to play with.

I hear Dr. Harmon say, "So why were you in your Dad's closet?"

"I don't know. I can't remember. I can only remember reaching up to the top shelf knocking over a few boxes and being scared as they hit the floor. I panicked as I tried quickly to pick everything up and figure out what came out of which box, and then that's when I saw a few birth certificates, social security cards, etc., but the next paper I picked up was titled DNA Results!!! I was young, but I knew what that meant."

"Sweeah, who's name is on the test? What do you see? Can you see a result?"

I'm trying to read the paper, but I'm scared because I hear Dad coming and calling my name.

"Sweeah, what the hell are you doing in her? Get out!! NOW!!!"

As I jump to my feet, I look at the paper in my hand and quickly see the name Elizabeth Evans…

"Sweeah…. Sweeah…. Wake up!"

The look on Dr. Harmon's face wasn't as bad as the last session, but he did look concerned. I was shaking and I woke up, I remember saying, "I'm sorry Dad.", which was weird, I've never had anxiety when I thought about my father. But once again, Dr. Harmon explained, yet again, what I uncovered. I was left once again feeling like my family is full of secrets, lies and betrayal.

Why would MeMe need a damn paternity test? I have to get to the bottom of this, and Dad knows, so yeah, what the fuck is going on in the damn Evans family!

This was enough for me today. I decided not to mention the new postcard I got this morning or the unexpected sex session I had with Shae'. I was mentally drained, and as I left the office, I hugged Dr. Monica and said, "It's always something," and she replied, "As long as we're alive, there's always gonna be something... It's how you handle the "something" that can make or break you. Remember that, and call me if you need me."

"I will", I said in a whisper.

The drive home was quiet. I didn't make a call, and I didn't play any music. I just wanted to talk to God. I was terrified, wondering if that paternity test could mean that Dad wasn't my dad, etc. And how was I going to approach this new situation?

Chapter 18

PLEASE GOD... SAVE HER!

I didn't have time to give it too much thought because my quiet car ride was interrupted by the ringing of my cell phone. It's Mook! Now what the fuck could she be possibly calling me for?

"Hello?" I answered aggressively.

"What??!! When did this happen?

"Where? Wait, what? Ok! Ok! What hospital is she going to? Ok! Bye!!!"

As I hung up the phone, all I can do is pray. God, please let her be okay. I can't lose anyone else that I love. My prayer is interrupted by the phone again. It's Perry, then Dad. I tell them both the same thing. I'm on my way to Einstein Hospital® right now. My blood pressure is through the roof, and I start to feel nauseous as I pull up to the ER with tears in my eyes and sprint to the Information Desk.

"Hello! My name is Sweeah Evans. I was told that my..."

"Sweeah! Over here!" It's Dad's voice. I turn around and run towards him.

"Dad! What happened? Is she okay? Tell me she's okay. Tell me they are both okay!"

"Yes, Sweeah. The doctor is in with her now. Come this way." Holding my hand, he escorts me to the room, where I see Mikaylah in the hospital bed with an IV in her arm and oxygen tubes in her nose.

"Oh My God! Mikaylah!!!" I say as I drop my bag on the chair and rush to be by her side. "Are you okay? Is the baby okay? What happened?"

"Mom. Yes, I'm okay. The baby is fine, too."

Just then, MeMe comes in the room, but the look on her face wasn't of fear or confusion. It was a familiar look that she gave me as if to warn me to stay calm. The look that lets me know that it's not the time or the place for my bullshit. So instantly, I thought Kyle was behind her, but I was dead wrong and literally at a loss for words when she stepped aside and said, "Hondo, this is Mikaylah's mom, Ms. Sweeah Evans. Sweeah, this is…"

"I know who it is, Mom," I said with my hand extended for a shake. "He's the baby's father."

Everyone looked around like 'how did you know'?

"Nice to finally meet you," I said.

His handshake was firm, and he made direct eye contact before pulling me in for a hug. He took a step back, smiled, and said, "Nice to finally meet you as well."

Just then, the doctor comes into the room, but as the door opens, I noticed two other gentlemen standing outside the room. Maybe they are his family members. I'll ask once the doctor finishes his exam. Turns out, Mikaylah was dehydrated, and her iron was low. She was also having Braxton-Hicks pains. Mom continued to give me the look, but I shot it right back at her, like OK! (Thanks to Perry, I had just found out about Hondo) but, MeMe, you have some explaining to do, because truth be told, y'all didn't seem like strangers. So, when the hell did she get introduced to the baby daddy?"

As soon as I part my lips to ask these questions, Dad comes over to me asking me how I was doing.

"How are you holding up?" he says as he hugs me tight.

"I'm okay, Dad. Just thankful that Mik and my grandson are both okay."

It was at this very moment that I decided to put a pause on what I just learned at therapy. This hug feels so damn soothing.... No matter what, he's MY Dad!" For now, anyway....

"What's your take on the young fella?" he asked, and before you can divert the question back to me, I just met him a few days ago, but Mikaylah begged your mother and me to keep quiet so she could formally introduce you guys at a dinner she was planning tomorrow. But then, this happened today. We like him." Dad said. He answered all my questions directly and without a bullshit conversation. School – family – work – sports, etc. I looked at Dad oddly because he usually doesn't curse.

We both laughed as he said, "Listen, the damage is already done, and in a few weeks, we will be having a bouncing baby boy. So, for the baby's sake, let's make this blended family work!"

I agreed with Dad and decided to do my best to make everything work out. Dad nudged me and then nodded in Hondo's direction. He was asking the doctor all the right questions, honestly questions that a woman would normally ask, which made me think his mother must've asked him these questions, etc. So, I walked over and asked him, "Hondo, is your mother here?"

"No, not yet, Ms. Evans. My parents are still in Miami."

"Mom!" Mikaylah calls out.

"Yes, Mik? Are you okay?"

"No. It hurts!"

Hondo pushes the button, and the doctor appears immediately and checks Mik telling her she's okay, that the Braxton-Hicks can vary. Some are mild, some not so much. As the doctor continues to inform the parents-to-be of what to expect, my phone rings. It's Ms. Carla.

"Sweeah, the hospital said we needed to be authorized to come up…"

"Authorized by whom?"

"I'm not sure. They said Mikaylah Evans is on a secured floor."

"Ok. Let me check this out." Just then, I left Mikaylah's room and realized that there were no other patients on the floors, and the two guys that I assumed were Hondo's uncles were walking the halls as if they were security. So, I headed back into the room and told MeMe to follow me back out into the hall.

"MeMe, what the hell is going on? Ms. Carla is trying to come upstairs, and they said she needs authorization."

"I'll let the nurse's station know it's okay for her to come up. Sweeah, I'll explain everything once we get home."

After a few moments, Ms. Carla exits the elevator, looking very frustrated. After checking in on Mikaylah and the baby, she exits the room, looking very confused.

"Who the hell wants to start explaining what's going on? Why is Mikaylah on a secured floor, and when did we find out who the baby's father was?"

Just when MeMe was about to give us both some insight, the two security dudes walked up and asked, Mikaylah's about to be discharged? and asked if we could all graciously follow them down to the secured exit. I was getting pissed, but MeMe seemed like she was unbothered, finally calling them by name. "Thanks, Torres. Thanks, Aaron."

Ms. Carla and I just rolled our eyes and followed their lead. MeMe informed us that Dad was coming down with Mikaylah and Hondo. She also used this time to tell us that she felt the same way days prior but said we would understand once she explained everything in detail. What the hell was going on?

Before the elevator doors opened, Ms. Carla made it clear that whatever was going on, Shae' and Mr. Amin were going to hit the fan.

Just then, I heard voices come through Aaron's earpiece. I couldn't hear what was being said to him, but I did hear him say, "No, ma'am. Kyle Evans isn't authorized, and if you'd like, tell him she's been discharged."

I look at Ms. Carla, and we both look at MeMe like... yeah, you have some serious explaining to do! When the doors opened, we were on a floor I'd never seen before, and we'd been coming to this hospital for years.

"Ladies, this way." Ms. Carla and I try to be upset, but these two guys are so polite and fine as fuck! We walk through the double doors where there's a black Escalade™ waiting for us. "Ladies?" Aaron said as he extended his hand to help us get into the truck. We drove about two doors down, and I saw Dad, Mikaylah, and

Hondo approach the truck. Mikaylah gets in and looks at her God Grandmother and me, and she knows we are pissed. Dad and Hondo get in, and the vehicle pulls off. In my head, I'm singing DMX™, 'y'all gonna make me lose my mind, up in here, up in here!'

Chapter 19

MEME... WE'RE LISTENING!

P ulling up to the house, I just burst out laughing as I see my car is already there. How the hell did that happen? Yet, from my peripheral view, I can see MeMe texting Kyle that Mikaylah's okay. But he's just saying, 'Why couldn't I come up to see my daughter?' MeMe said there was a limit on visitors and Mikaylah would call him later.

Then we exit, and Ms. Carla is on her phone with Amin, saying, 'I'll fill y'all in later.'

"Thank you," Mikaylah says as Hondo walks her to the door. Once inside, he politely asks me if it's okay to escort her to her room.

"Yes, baby. It's fine." I say to him as he oh so gently helps her up the stairs.

"Wait," Dad says as he gives her one last hug. Dad excuses himself, saying he is going back home to call Mr. Mason back. He said today's events nearly gave him a heart attack, and he needed to go rest up. As he left, we could see Torres and Aaron still standing out front, on guard, looking fine as hell.

"Elizabeth Evans! In the kitchen NOW!" was the last thing I heard before seeing Ms. Carla power walk to the sink. I quickly followed behind her, halfway rolling my eyes at MeMe. In a whisper, MeMe motions her hands, "Okay... okay... Would you calm down?"

"MeMe, how long have you been sneaking around with Mikaylah and Hondo?"

"Sweets, listen, a few weeks ago..."

"A few weeks!!" I yelled. "Mom, really?!"

"Sweeah, are you gonna let me finish?" she said, clenching her teeth.

I throw up my hands and say nothing.

Meanwhile, Ms. Carla watched the doorway to ensure no one walked in on our heated conversation.

A few weeks ago, I overheard Mikaylah on the phone saying, "I love you too. I'll see you again tomorrow." I knew it wasn't one of us, so I asked who was on the phone, making plans to see her tomorrow. She said, "MeMe, promise you won't tell my mom. Because I'm planning a dinner for my mom to meet Hondo and explain how all this came to be." But I told her since I knew he was coming; I wasn't waiting until the dinner. Once we met him and talked, Dad and I were so impressed that we just agreed to keep quiet.

"I agree he's definitely a gentleman, but what the hell

was all that about at the hospital?"

"The hospital?" Ms. Carla said, "Girl, we still have security right outside."

"Oh yeah," MeMe says with a smirk. "Torres and Aaron are his personal bodyguards. His family is crazy rich! His dad is a successful businessman, and Hondo is his only child; they are very protective of him. And clearly, they aren't taking any chances on their first grandchild."

Ms. Carla and I shake our heads in disbelief as there is a knock on the kitchen door.

It's Aaron, who I swear looks like a fine ass Saudi King - LAWD HAVE MERCY! He's somewhat smiling as he asked me to please come to the front door.

"Ok," I say to him. "This isn't over, MeMe."

Walking to the front door, I exhale and laugh, seeing this fool, Perry, with his arms up, begging to be frisked. "Get in here, dummy!" I say, snatching his arm.

"Sweeah, what the fuck is going on in this jawn?"

"It's a long story." I say, "But Mik and the baby are okay, thank God."

Just then Hondo comes down the stairs and Perry asks, 'what the hell is going on?'

With his right hand extended to Perry, he says, "What's up? How are you? Uncle Perry, right? Mikaylah has told me all about you. I'm Hondo, her boyfriend, father of the baby, Joaquin."

Jaws drop as we all say, "Wait… y'all chose a name?"

"Sorry, Mom." I heard a faint voice coming down the stairs. "We were going to share this news at the dinner. I hope you're not mad." She said while rubbing her stomach.

"No, Mikaylah, sweetie. I'm not mad, just shocked. But I love it! It's a strong name for a strong boy!"

Yeah, that's what I said to Hondo. The entire name is strong! Joaquin Khameron Guzman.

"Awww…" Perry said, "Your brother is going to be so excited. Uncle Khamm has a namesake.

"Mom, I thought about his middle name a lot, and although I miss KJ, I can't allow my son to keep my dad's name with how he's treating you."

"Mikaylah, I understand. The name you both chose is perfect." I hugged her tight, and everyone felt the words 'I love you.'

"Well, hey, Miss Thang!" Perry says with his arms outstretched for a hug. "Girl, what's wrong with you scaring us like that? I should beat y'all's butts!"

We all laugh as Perry looks at Aaron and Torres, "like all y'all's butts."

Chapter 20

DNA! NO, HE CAN'T BE!

"Mom, were you cooking anything? We are starving!"

"No, no, Mik. I'm sure your mom is tired. It's been a long day for all of us. If you're up to it, why don't we all go out for that dinner we were planning?"

"Okay. I'm down." Mik says.

"Mom? What about you?"

"Choose the spot, Ms. Evans. Wherever you want to go. Ruth Chris®, Moshulu®, Steak 48®."

Perry's stupid ass is talking under his breath, 'like – my investigators clearly missed a lot of information on the background check."

"Yes. They clearly fumbled the ball."

As we head out the door, Ms. Carla's phone rings. "Hey, Shae'? What's up, baby?"

Not knowing what he was saying on the other end, I stood in the room so I could hear what Ms. Carla was saying. I start to smile just thinking about him fucking me all crazy on his mother's floor. My Gawd! I must've drifted off because I now hear Mikaylah say,

"Great! Now you can meet my God Dad, too."

"Shit! Shae' is coming? What the fuck?"

Perry's face was like, 'Bitch, get a grip on yourself!'

As we drove to the Moshulu®, I looked around, and something seemed off. I know it's a weekday, but the parking lot seemed empty. But I did notice one car, and so did Perry, as he slightly pinched my leg, saying, "Gurl... look at Shae'." I popped Perry's hand like, 'Boy, calm down! Trust me, I see all of his fine ass, and next to him is Mr. Amin."

We pull up to the dock/curb and begin to exit the trucks. That's when I nearly died as Aaron helped me out the car door. "Watch your step," he says oh so gently. But then Shae' says, "Thanks, man. I got her from here. His touch went all through me. I was praying nobody could pick up on our damn chemistry. And then I heard, "Hey! You must be Shae', Mikaylah's God Dad! I'm Hondo. Her boyfriend and soon-to-be Joaquin's dad."

"Joaquin?" Shae' said as he looked at me.

"Yes, sir. Joaquin." Still shaking his hand firmly.

"Well, okay then. Yes, I'm Shae'. Nice to finally meet you."

"Likewise," Hondo said as he escorted everyone to the boat's ramp.

Ms. Carla and MeMe were now focused on how empty it was the closer we got to the door of the Moshulu®.

"Are they open?" MeMe asked.

"I don't know." Ms. Carla replied. "Seems like we're the only ones here."

At that point, Mikaylah said, "It's open, but only for us. Hondo bought it out for the night.

"WAIT! WHAT?!" we all said, confused.

"Bought out what with what?" Perry said. "He bought out the entire ship restaurant?"

"Yes," Mikaylah said, smiling.

"Mom, MeMe, GG Carla, can y'all just go inside and close y'all's mouths?"

"Okay," I said while shaking my fucking head. How can he afford to buy out a ship for the night?

Perry, being Perry, replies, "Clearly his daddy is a millionaire! Good job, Mikaylah," he said as he opened the door. "Let's go y'all! We got this jawn all to ourselves!" Perry said while switching past Aaron and Torres, who were paying him no mind.

Once inside, we noticed more security men. They had also made one huge table for us. Mik, MeMe, Ms. Carla, Shae', Mr. Amin, Perry, myself, and Hondo. As we all sit down, I hear, "Mommy, Mommy." It's Khamm and my dad.

Hondo had sent for them, and they walked in happy as hell; so much for Dad being so tired. As we sat and mingled, we ordered damn near everything off the menu, and the atmosphere was so joyous and peaceful.

We started talking about the upcoming baby shower, and Hondo said he was so excited to meet the rest of the family, and we said likewise. But I didn't know that the extra seats would soon be filled by…

Mikaylah's phone rings, and she says, "Yes. Let her up. Thank you." Perry looks at me as I say, "Mik, who was that?" But before she could open her mouth, Mook walked in. I nearly jumped out of my chair to beat her ass, but I had to remember that nobody knew about her and Kyle besides Perry. So, the genuine hugs and kisses she got from everyone made me sick. So, to keep my cool, I just waved and started laughing at the bullshit Perry was saying.

"You want me to kick her overboard? Do you want me to shank the bitch? She has a lot of nerve coming up in this jawn!"

"Perry! Please calm down… Remember, nobody knows!"

"Sweeah," he said, "You are better than me because…"

I stopped him. "NOPE! I'm not better than you. Trust me. I want to fuck her up, but my kids are here and trust me for the son I lost because of her, I'm gonna get her back. But look at Mikaylah. Look at my Mom and Dad, etc. I have to shake it off. Everyone knows how close Mik and Mook are. So, it's okay, for now, that is…"

Just then, I excused myself from the table and headed to the ladies' room. I didn't make it two feet before I heard Shae' say, "Khamm, my man, walk with me." I laughed on the inside because he was using Khamm to follow me. Once out of sight from the guests, I said, "Khamm, are you following mommy?" With a tummy tickle. "Nooooo" he said laughing, "But I do need to pee" he said. So, Shae' opened the door, reminded Khamm to flush and wash his hands.

As soon as Khamm went in, I peeked around the wall to make sure no one else was heading to the bathroom. That's when I felt Shae's fingers slip past my waistband and into my panties. He's behind me and quickly places his left hand around my neck and his right fingers into my pussy, gently bending me over, but thrusting his fingers inside my volcanic walls which now has warm lava and not a moment too soon. We hear Khamm singing as he washes his hands, so we knew time was up.

"Mommy, you waited for me too?"

"Oh yes!" I said as Shae's nasty ass licks his fingers, then says, "Khamm, hold up… let me wash my hands. Somehow, they became sticky."

While Shae' washed his hands, I bent down and hugged Khamm.

"You know I love you, right, Khameron?"

"Mom, yes. But why are you saying my entire name?"

We laughed as Shae' came out. "I love that name, and you're getting older. The girls might want to call you Khameron." Khamm's face lit up at the mention of little girls liking him.

"Okay! Okay! I guess my name is cool."

"My man!" Shae' said, reaching up for a high five.

Just then, out of nowhere, Perry pops up. Shae' and Khamm head back to the table.

"What's up, bitch?" I say to Perry.

We both laugh briefly because Perry could sense something had just happened.

"Stay focused." He said. "I just overhead ya' mom on the phone saying, 'Yes. Let them up' and bitch, I didn't know who THEM was... I pray it ain't Kyle," he says, rolling his eyes.

"Naw... Mikaylah ain't fucking with Kyle, and before I could get my next sentence out, I heard Khamm yelling, "Amiyah! Aunt Lonna!!" everyone extended more hugs and kisses as they met Hondo.

Again, Perry and I begin to play fight each other while asking each other, 'Is this shit for real?' As we walk back to the table, smiling to blend in. I got a text from Shae'. "I need you bad. Hilton after this. Room 1212."

As Lonna extends a warm welcome to Hondo. Amiyah runs over to me and jumps into my arms. I must admit that I miss my niece so damn much. It seems like forever since I've seen her. Lonna's nut ass has her with Stix and Yasmine more than me, and honestly, that fucks with me. I squat down to Amiyah's height and tell her she's gonna help me at the baby shower, and we can wear matching colors. As she laughs with excitement, I can see Lonna approaching Shae', who gives her a hug and a peck on her lips. I smile because he never rinsed his mouth from licking his fingers although he washed his hands. Yup!! I'm Petty LaBelle!!! But this just pushes me to be EXTRA nasty tonight when I'm fucking her husband all crazy. It's time for a Disney® redo!

Overall, the evening was amazing, minus Lonna and Mook. I was happy to see MeMe and Dad so happy. Honestly, nobody really cares that Mikaylah and Hondo are gonna be teen parents. Clearly, they are gonna have a shit load of support. I mean, at this point, it is what it is. And the evening was drama-free…or so I thought.

As the evening starts to wind down and the dessert is served, I once again take an overall look at my family, and out of nowhere, BOOOOM!!!! My head starts pounding. *Now brace yourselves…even I didn't see this coming.* BOOM!! A Flash! I'm back at therapy, hearing Dr. Harmon and Dr. Monica explain to me that one of my childhood memories was of MeMe, Dad, Ms. Carla, and Mr. Amin having a damn orgy/swingers night and me hearing them argue about it in the kitchen when I was about seven years old, but I couldn't remember the details.

BOOM! I grabbed my head and the two things I heard was Perry asking me if I was okay and the next thing was the seven-year-old me hearing Ms. Carla say, "either of you could be Shae's father. No one has to know, and Mr. Amin agrees to raise him regardless.

Perry looks at me, and I say, "Get me out of here *NOW*!!" My immediate thoughts were, 'I've been fucking my brother!' and why would they allow Lonna to marry him? But I remembered that Mom had Lonna before she met Dad, so even if Shae' is Dad's, he and Lonna are unrelated. But I would be his little sister!!!

Perry and I excused ourselves as I feel like I'm about to throw up. It was perfect timing, as dinner was ending. Mook had already snuck out earlier, and security was escorting everyone out. I came up with a story to swap rides, so Dad and Khamm rode back with Mikaylah and Hondo, and Perry and I took Dad's car. I kissed Mik and said, "Give me an hour with your uncle, OK?" Laughing, she said, "Okay. One hour." I sat silently as we pulled off, and I started meditating. I'm trying my best to dig deep and be sure that's what I heard Ms. Carla say in the kitchen.

Perry pulls the car over down the street at Penns Landing, and I jump out, falling to my knees like, 'What the fuck is going on??!!'

"Bitch!! Get up!!!" he says. "Get the FUCK UP! What is it now?" he continued, with his hand extended to pull me up. And since he knows damn near everything else, I just blurt it out. "Shae' might be my FUCKING BROTHER!!!"

Made in the USA
Middletown, DE
25 August 2024

59241412R00086